THE WATERFALL

SECOND CHANCES
BOOK ONE

J.N. KING
CASSANDRA DOON

Age is just a number
Love knows no bounds

1

____

Piper

The chime of the café door announced my arrival. This Pavlovian cue stirred within me an immediate sense of reprieve. I glided to my customary spot, a secluded table by the window whose view afforded me glimpses of humanity in its unguarded moments, all while cradling the sanctuary of solitude. The worn wood of the chair greeted me like an old friend, and it creaked a familiar tune in the backdrop of frothing espressos and subdued conversations.

I carefully unfolded the napkin. Unlike the frenzied ballet of office colleagues dodging the clock's tyranny, I basked in the full breadth of my allotted freedom. The café's proximity to work—just a stone's throw away—granted me this privilege, one I cherished with the reverence of a secret treasure.

With each passing second, I could feel the tendrils of

tranquillity weaving through the frayed edges of my consciousness, stitching together the fragments left by morning's demands. Here, ensconced in my alcove of escape, I allowed myself to drift on waves of thought, contemplating the mosaic of experiences that had led me to this juncture.

"Taking a moment for yourself, Piper?" The barista's light and friendly voice punctuated my reverie without intrusion.

"Every day," I replied, my tone laced with the softness of appreciation. "The tiny islands of peace make the ocean of chaos navigable."

A smile played on my lips as I leaned back, watching the world whirl outside the window. Tomorrow, the scene would shift dramatically; today, however, was a testament to the routines that had anchored me through seasons of change. As the threads of my past wove into the fabric of my future, I knew unequivocally that this quiet corner would forever hold the essence of my metamorphosis.

The clink of the tall glass meeting the saucer echoed faintly, a prelude to indulgence. My fingers curled around the coolness of the caramel frappe, condensation beading like tiny jewels against my skin. I lifted it, amber liquid swirling, the extra shot of caramel bleeding into the frosty blend—a sweet, viscous symphony to my palate. With each sip, the richness of the flavour coaxed a sigh from my lips, the saccharine solace a stark contrast to the morning's bitter rush of deadlines and pencilled sketches.

I set the glass down, taking note of the cheese toastie placed neatly beside it—the golden crust winking up at me, the cheese peeking from within like molten treasure. It was simplicity itself, a nod to comfort that never demanded more than what it gave: warmth and satisfaction. Biting into it, the crunch resonated, a sound almost as gratifying as the taste. The familiarity of the meal was grounding, an edible echo of consistency in my ever-shifting world.

Outside the café's embrace, the summer heat pressed its claim upon the city. It lay heavy upon the pavements, a blanket woven from the sun's loom. June unfurled its fiery temperament across the sky, painting strokes of languor onto the day's canvas. I could feel the heat even through the glass, watching as people passed by in a mirage-like dance, their forms rippling with the distortion of rising warmth from the sunbaked streets.

This insistent heat whispered promises of distant shores, the caress of ocean breezes and the kiss of salt-water mist. The yearning for escape billowed within me, a sail caught in the gale of my desires. Each bead of sweat that traced down someone's brow outside spoke of the need for respite—a universal call to which my heart thrummed.

"Hot enough for you, Piper?" the barista quipped, his smile reaching his eyes as he wiped down the counter with a practised swirl of his cloth.

"Scorching," I replied, the corner of my mouth lifting. "Makes you wish you could dissolve into the foam of a breaking wave, doesn't it?"

"Can't say I've had the pleasure," he chuckled before moving off to attend to another patron—a tourist, perhaps, unaccustomed to our local inferno.

Alone again with my thoughts, I allowed them to

wander, to trace the contours of my anticipation. Family and friends, with their well-meaning concern, hovered on the periphery of my mind, their voices an affectionate murmur that I gently pushed aside. They did not understand the wealth of solitude, the affluence in moments spent with oneself, nor the treasure trove of discovery that awaited in the vast expanse of being alone.

I swept my fingers over the surface of the caramel frappe glass, tracing a path through the condensation. The chill against my skin contrasted with the sweltering heat that clung to the air outside the café's welcoming embrace. Tomorrow, the sultry grip of the city would be a world away; twenty-four hours from now, I'd be surrendering to the skies, an airborne pilgrim en route to O'ahu.

The thought sent a shiver of excitement spiralling down my spine, mingling with the nervous flutter in my stomach. It had been two years since I last stepped foot on a plane, two years since I allowed myself the luxury of new horizons. How peculiar it was that the vastness of the sky could feel both like an old friend and a stranger.

This journey was more than a mere change of scenery or a reprieve from the relentless pace of urban life. It was the inaugural act of reclaiming my narrative after the ink had dried on the divorce papers. Lucas's absence was no longer a void but a space cleared for possibility. And I intended to fill it with the richness of unaccompanied exploration—my first solo travel venture.

I squinted into the sun-drenched street as I envisioned the lush landscapes and turquoise waters that awaited me. O'ahu promised a wealth of experiences, a balm for the soul that had grown weary of chasing deadlines and accolades. There, among the whispering palms and rolling waves, I would seek out the wealth that mattered—measured not by bank accounts and portfolios but by moments of profound solitude and self-discovery.

I closed my eyes, letting the buzz of the café fade into the background. Piper Robinson, the illustrator who once found comfort in the lines she drew on paper, was ready to sketch a new chapter where each step, breath, and heartbeat was a note in a symphony of self-reliance. Family ties and societal expectations were the undercurrents beneath a surface that I alone would navigate.

Austin

"ARE YOU READY?" THE QUESTION HUNG IN THE AIR, spoken in Killian's rich baritone that echoed off the stark walls of our shared dorm room. His voice was a familiar sound that had become the soundtrack to my academic life. He was more than just my roommate; he was my confidant, my partner in crime. We were comrades on and off the football field, our companionship forged amidst gruelling practices under scorching suns and solidified by a shared scholarship that had brought us to this prestigious college.

Our bond was an unspoken agreement, a mutual understanding born of countless shared experiences. We were on the precipice of yet another thrilling escapade. Our hard work and dedication had paid off, securing us coveted spots at an elite sports camp in the tropical paradise of O'ahu for the summer holidays.

These camps served as our sanctuary, our refuge from the rigours of academia. They were places where we could channel our boundless energy and fervour into something productive while letting loose and indulging in much-needed relaxation. The prospect of partying beneath the vibrant Hawaiian skies, with its tapestry of stars overhead and pushing our bodies to their absolute limits during intense training sessions, was exhilarating.

It felt like we'd discovered some secret recipe for happiness - a way to balance work with play, to have our cake and relish every bite too."All packed," I replied with a nod towards my suitcase, bulging at its seams from all it contained. A sense of finality washed over me as I zipped it shut.

"Matt should be here in about 15 minutes." Our friend Matt was akin to human clockwork—always reliable when providing rides, especially when those involved trips to airports for exciting adventures.

We were scheduled to rendezvous with the rest of our motley crew – fellow athletes who shared our insatiable thirst for fun and fitness – at gate 7. The anticipation was palpable, buzzing between us like a live wire, sending excitement dancing through the room.

With one last lingering glance at my humble abode, I hoisted my bag onto my shoulder, feeling the familiar strain of its weight against my muscles. The door closed behind me with a weighty click that echoed in the silence. This summer promised an avalanche of fun and excitement; I could hardly contain my eagerness for it all to begin.

2

Piper

The reflection in the mirror stared back at me, my eyes bright with the promise of a new beginning. I adjusted my scarf one last time, savouring the anticipation that danced within me. My suitcase waited by the door, a silent companion ready for the journey ahead. Today marked the start of my adventure to Oahu—a journey that signified more than just miles travelled. It was a declaration of independence, a vow to embrace life on my terms.

The taxi ride to London Heathrow was a blur of city lights and quiet contemplation. As the car wound its way through the familiar streets, I found solace in the gentle hum of the engine and the rhythmic cadence of tyres against asphalt. My thoughts were a tapestry of memories and dreams woven together by the threads of anticipation.

At the airport, the bustling crowds moved with

purpose, each traveller a story in motion. I navigated through the sea of faces, my heart beating faster with each step. The weight of my decision to disconnect from work settled into a comfortable resolve. This trip was about reclaiming my narrative, free from the demands and deadlines that had once defined me.

The flight itself was a cocoon of tranquillity. I nestled into my seat, letting the gentle hum of the plane lull me into a sense of peace. The book in my hands was a portal to another world, its pages turning slowly as I was lost in its embrace, and hours slipped away, marked by the rise and fall of my breathing as I drifted in and out of sleep. The promise I had made to myself—not to touch anything work-related—felt liberating. This journey was mine, and I intended to savour every moment.

WHEN WE FINALLY TOUCHED DOWN IN OAHU, THE AIR WAS thick with the scent of salt and sunshine. The airport buzzed with the energy of arrivals and departures, a symphony of beginnings and farewells. I stepped off the plane, feeling the warmth of the island wrap around me like a welcome embrace. In the arrivals hall, a man held a sign with my name, his smile a beacon of hospitality. "Ms. Robinson?" he called, his voice carrying overcrowd's din. "That's me," I replied, walking towards him. The reality of my new adventure settled over me, a thrilling mixture of excitement and calm. "Welcome to Oahu," he said warmly. "I'll be taking you to the Ocean Valley Resort."

The drive to the resort was a feast for the senses. Palm

trees lined the roads, their fronds swaying gently in the breeze. The ocean sparkled under the midday sun, waves lapping against the shore with a timeless rhythm. I drank in the sights, feeling the stresses of the past year melt away.

The Ocean Valley Resort was everything I had hoped for and more. Nestled just a stone's throw from the beach, it promised a sanctuary of luxury and tranquillity. The resort boasted an array of amenities—bars, clubs, sports activities, restaurants, shops, yoga, pilates, a spa, and more. It was a haven designed for indulgence and relaxation, and I intended to immerse myself fully.

As I checked in and was shown to my room, I felt a surge of gratitude. This time was a gift to myself, a period of reflection and renewal. The room was spacious and elegantly appointed, with a balcony offering a breathtaking ocean view. I stepped outside, letting the sea breeze kiss my skin as I closed my eyes and breathed deeply. This was not a midlife crisis but a deliberate choice to seize and enjoy life.

After a year of navigating the complexities of divorce, I was ready to focus on myself and what I truly wanted. This trip was a step towards planning the next chapter of my life, filled with purpose and passion. I unpacked my suitcase, each item a reminder of my commitment to self-discovery. Comfortable clothes for yoga and pilates, books that promised journeys of the mind, and a journal to capture my thoughts and dreams. I had no intention of leaving the resort much; it offered everything I needed to rejuvenate and reflect.

As the sun dipped below the horizon, painting the sky

in hues of orange and pink, I felt a sense of calm wash over me. This was my time, a sacred interlude to reconnect with myself. I was ready to embrace the wealth of solitude and the richness of new experiences. The next chapter of my life awaited, and I was poised to write it with intention and joy.

Tomorrow, I would explore the resort, indulge in its luxuries, and let the island's magic weave its spell. But tonight, I would simply be—present in the moment, savouring the beauty of now. This was a journey of self-discovery, where each step, breath, and heartbeat was a note in a symphony of self-reliance.

The room was a sanctuary of calm, filled with the soft hum of the air conditioning and the distant murmur of the ocean. I opened my suitcase and began to unpack, savouring the ritual. Each item I placed in the dresser drawers or hung in the closet felt like a piece of myself being carefully arranged into this new chapter: a flowing sundress, perfect for evening strolls along the beach, comfortable sandals for wandering the resort, and a swimsuit that whispered promises of lazy afternoons by the pool.

* * *

THE ACT OF UNPACKING FELT LIKE SHEDDING THE LAYERS of my past, making space for the new experiences that awaited. With my belongings neatly stowed away, I decided to explore the resort.

The Ocean Valley Resort was vast, a sprawling oasis of luxury and tranquillity. I stepped out of my room and warmly embraced the island's tropical air. The pathways were lined with lush greenery and vibrant flowers, their colours a feast for the eyes. I wandered through the resort, letting my senses guide me.

The first stop was the spa, a haven of relaxation with its promise of massages and treatments designed to rejuvenate the body and soul. From there, I meandered to the fitness centre. At this state-of-the-art facility, guests could engage in everything from yoga and pilates to high-intensity interval training. I made a mental note to sign up for a few classes.

Next, I was by the pool area, where sun loungers beckoned, and the shimmering water invited a dip. Nearby, a beach bar served tropical cocktails, and I could hear the faint sound of music mingling with the laughter of guests enjoying their day. The resort's restaurants offered a tantalising array of cuisines, each promising a culinary adventure I was eager to embark on.

As I continued to explore, I realised just how expansive the resort was. There were bars and clubs, shops filled with local crafts and souvenirs, and even a small cinema. Despite my best efforts, I couldn't see it all in one go. There was too much to take in, too many hidden corners and unexpected delights waiting to be discovered.

Eventually, I found myself near the tennis courts, where the sound of rackets striking balls echoed in the air. Then, I noticed the banners proclaiming the Ocean Valley Athletes Program. Curious, I moved closer, observing the athletes practising with a dedication that spoke of more than just vacation leisure. The program seemed to be some kind of sports camp for athletes, their intense focus and disciplined routines hinting at a deeper purpose.

I wondered what the program entailed and who participated. Was it for professional athletes seeking a retreat to hone their skills or for amateurs looking to elevate their game? What kind of training did they undergo, and who were the coaches guiding them? The questions buzzed in my mind as I watched a group of athletes cool down after a rigorous session, their camaraderie and shared purpose evident in their interactions.

Austin

THE BUZZ OF EXCITEMENT HUMMED IN MY VEINS AS WE navigated through the bustling airport towards gate 7. Each step felt like a leap closer to the adventure we'd been eagerly anticipating ever since we received that life-changing sponsorship offer. The mere thought of Hawaii was enough to set my heart racing with anticipation. Killian and Matt were beside me, their laughter and banter filling the air with camaraderie that only true friends could share. We were like a trio of kids on Christmas morning, giddy and unable to contain our anticipation for what lay ahead.

"Can you believe we're doing this?" I couldn't help but marvel aloud as we reached our gate, the reality of our journey sinking in with each passing moment. Always with contagious confidence, Killian slung an arm around my shoulder and gave me a playful shove. "Believe it,

Austin! We're about to take Hawaii by storm." Matt's eyes sparkled with unbridled excitement as he nodded in agreement. "I can already picture us on the beach, soaking up the sun and living our best lives."

With our boarding passes in hand, we joined the queue of fellow travellers, a diverse tapestry of athletes from all walks of life, each bound together by a shared passion for sports and a hunger for success. It was a humbling sight, knowing that we were about to embark on this journey alongside many other talented individuals with their dreams and aspirations.

As we settled into our seats on the plane, the engines roared to life, a symphony of anticipation for the adventures that awaited us on the other side of the ocean. I couldn't help but feel a swell of pride and gratitude for the opportunity to represent myself, my team, and my country on the international stage. With a deep breath and a heart full of excitement, I leaned back in my seat, ready to ride the wave of this once-in-a-lifetime opportunity, knowing that no matter what lay ahead, I had my best friends by my side, ready to conquer whatever challenges came our way.

As we settled for the journey, the anticipation of our adventure in Hawaii bubbled over into excited chatter between Killian and Matt. Our dreams of playing football professionally felt closer than ever, and the prospect of spending the summer in paradise was just the cherry on top. "So, boys, ready to make some waves in Hawaii?" I grinned, already imagining the pristine beaches and lush landscapes awaiting us. Killian, with his dark hair and piercing green eyes, flashed a cocky smirk. "You bet your ass, Austin. They have some serious talent, but none can match us." Matt, his All-American charm shining through, chimed in, "Absolutely! But let's not forget why we're there. We're there to train, improve, and show the world what we're made of." I nodded in agreement but couldn't resist adding, "Of course, but that doesn't mean we can't have a little fun, right? I mean, it's Hawaii, after all. We've gotta soak up every bit of the experience." Killian's grin widened, a mischievous glint in his eye. "Oh, don't you worry, Austin. I've heard the parties in Hawaii are legendary. And it's gonna be unforgettable with the three of us there." I couldn't help but chuckle at his enthusiasm, knowing full well that Killian's reputation preceded him, especially regarding parties. But amidst the excitement of the trip, I couldn't shake the sense of determination burning within me. "Let's not lose sight of why we're there," I said, my tone more serious now. "We've got a chance to train with some of the best athletes in the world. We need to make the most of every opportunity." Killian and Matt nodded in agreement, the gravity of our mission settling over us like a cloak. We were here to chase our dreams, to push ourselves to the limit, and to show the world what we were made of.

BUT AS THE PLANE SOARED TOWARDS OUR DESTINATION, I couldn't help but feel a surge of excitement coursing through me. Hawaii awaited, a paradise filled with endless possibilities and adventures just waiting to be had. And with my two best friends by my side, I knew that whatever the summer held in store for us, we would face it together, united in our pursuit of greatness.

Stepping off the plane and into the warm embrace of Oahu's tropical air felt like a dream. The scent of saltwater mingled with the fragrant blooms of exotic flowers, enveloping us in a sense of paradise that seemed almost too good to be true. But there was no denying it – we had arrived, and the adventure of a lifetime awaited us.

As we gathered our luggage and made our way through the bustling airport, I couldn't help but be swept away by the vibrant energy pulsating through the air. Everywhere I looked, there were athletes from all corners of the globe, their excitement palpable as they prepared to embark on their journeys.

Amidst the hustle and bustle, I was suddenly drawn to a figure moving gracefully through the crowd. She was unlike anyone I had ever seen – her long, dark brown hair cascading down her back in loose waves, her bright eyes sparkling with a warmth that seemed to light up the entire room. There was an air of elegance about her, a sense of confidence that drew me in like a moth to a flame.

Time seemed to stand still momentarily as I watched her, captivated by her beauty. But then, reality came crashing back in as I felt a tug on my arm and heard my friends calling out to me, urging me to hurry so we wouldn't miss the shuttle to camp. Reluctantly tearing my gaze away from the mysterious woman, I followed Killian and Matt towards the shuttle, my heart still racing with the memory of her presence.

But when I turned back for one last glance, she was nowhere to be found, lost amidst the sea of faces in the bustling airport. Disappointment gnawed at me as I settled into my seat on the shuttle, her image still lingering in my mind. But as we pulled away from the airport and began our journey towards camp, I couldn't shake the feeling that our encounter was just the beginning of something unexpected that would change the course of my summer in ways I could never have imagined.

3

Piper

The night draped O'ahu in its sumptuous velvet darkness, and there I was, a solitary figure weaving my thread of introspection into the island's vibrant tapestry. The resort restaurant, a tableau of soft lights and murmured conversations, cradled me at a table that seemed destined for one. I had chosen this spot deliberately, a cozy nook where the water's gentle ripple could be my clandestine companion. With each dish that arrived—a mosaic of local flavours—I indulged in the island's bountiful embrace, savouring the tang of sea salt on fresh poke and the sweet caress of papaya upon my tongue.

I had been lost in the pages of a novel, its characters' dilemmas mirroring my quiet contemplation of life's intricate dance. But as I turned another page, my sanctuary of solitude was breached by an escalating cacophony that invaded like curious tendrils of sound. Reluctantly, I lifted my gaze from the fictional world that held me captive. My senses sharpened, tuning in to the source of this unwelcome symphony.

With a soft sigh, I marked my place in the book with a slender finger and peered over the rim of my book to witness the source of this disruption. The athletes from the tennis courts, their figures still adorned with the sheen of exertion, were now staking claim to the tables surrounding me. A captivating tableau unfolded before me as they fragmented into smaller gatherings, each a self-contained world within the grand universe of their collective. The way they positioned themselves seemed to sketch out unseen borders, intimate clusters shaped by the unseen threads of shared pasts or silent pacts.

The dynamics of their interactions piqued my curiosity; a living tableau of social navigation paralleled my journey through life's vast network of relationships. Each cluster was an island, and I wondered about the currents between them—the undercurrents of competition, loyalty, and perhaps the subtle push and pull of regional pride.

But there was one who drew my focus like a beacon in a sea of faces. He stood slightly apart, his height a towering testament to genetics blessed by the gods of sport. His physique was a contrast study—broad shoulders tapering into a narrow waist. These muscles spoke of disciplined training and youthful resilience. His hair, the colour of the sun, caught the light in a way that it appeared almost fluid, a cascade of waves that framed his face with an effortless charm.

He was youth personified, a sculpture of potential and

vigour that seemed almost palpable across the distance. A flicker of warmth sparked within me as I observed him—a recognition of something familiar. This type had once been the subject of girlish daydreams. Those days felt like a lifetime ago, yet here he was, a spectre of youthful allure, reminding me of the fervour of early passions.

His movements were graceful, an echo of the athleticism that no doubt dominated his existence, and I found myself momentarily entranced. There was an ease to him, a fluidity that belied the strength evident in every line of his body. I estimated him to be in the nascent bloom of adulthood—20, perhaps 21. The world was still a place of boundless opportunity for him, each decision a brush stroke on the canvas of his life.

As laughter and chatter swirled like the delicate dance of sea foam upon the shore, my gaze lingered on him—the athlete whose presence seemed to echo the carefree exuberance of my younger years. A pang of nostalgia swept through me, a tide tugging at old memories: the rush of a first crush, the thrill of a playful pursuit, the ache of youthful desire. He was the archetype, the embodiment of those reckless heartbeats I once knew, the type I would have chased down school corridors or yearned to sway under the dim lights of a gymnasium adorned with streamers and shy hopes.

He was all the dreams I'd penned in hidden pages, wrapped in the raw promise of youth—a promise I had tucked away along with those diaries. Would I have traded a piece of myself back then, a kidney or a slice of my soul, just for the brush of his hand against mine in rhythm to a long-forgotten song? Perhaps. It was easy to be bold when the heart was unscarred, fearless in its ignorance of time's relentless march.

I was ensnared in this reverie, a silent sonnet to the past, when the unexpected happened. Alight with the same fervent spark, his eyes found mine across the crowded space. The connection was instantaneous, a bolt of lightning that bridged the gap between our separate worlds. His smile—oh, that smile! It was a sunburst, radiant and warm, unfurled something within me. This blush bloomed like the hibiscus flowers dotting the resort's paths.

My lips curved in response, reflecting his joy, but it was a fleeting moment—an ember quickly smothered by self-awareness. I turned my face away, letting my hair cascade like a curtain to shield me from the intensity of his gaze. In that exchange, there was a whisper of possibilities, a murmur of what could be if the world were different—if I were different. But in the sanctuary of my solitude, I grappled with the complexities of such thoughts, the weight of years and experiences that separated us.

"Focus, Piper," I chided myself silently, my voice the anchor I sought to steady the ship of my wandering mind. Yet even as I returned to the safety of my book, the text blurred before my eyes, sentences melting into a sea of ink as his image lingered on the periphery of my vision.

Austin

MY GAZE WAS DRAWN LIKE A MAGNET, PULLED ACROSS THE room to a woman whose allure eclipsed the very essence of what I had known beauty to be. She sat there, an enigma wrapped in elegance, her physique a testament to years of discipline—a symphony of strength and femininity that harmonised in a form so intoxicating it seemed to hum softly beneath my skin. With each subtle movement, she wove grace into the air around her, commanding attention without even a whisper of effort.

In the sea of digital obsessions, she emerged as an island of timeless allure, her eyes not glued to a screen but dancing over the pages of a book cradled gently in her hand. More than any other, this detail ensnared me—her disinterest in the virtual world hinting at a depth of character I found profoundly alluring. Was she a throwback to a bygone era or a renegade choosing to exist on her terms? Her age was a mystery, veiled behind the poise of her posture and the serene confidence in her gaze. She was a masterpiece sculpted by the years yet untouched by time's unforgiving hand.

As if orchestrating her private symphony of flavours, she daintily picked through an array of dishes spread before her, sampling each with an explorer's curiosity and a connoisseur's palate. Her fingers, slender and sure, danced from plate to plate, a visual melody of indulgence and restraint. In this culinary exploration, she did not simply eat; she savoured, as though every bite was a note in a grander composition, a journey traversed upon the landscape of her tongue.

"Earth to Austin." The sudden nudge at my side was Killian's doing, his elbow a grounding rod that yanked me back from the brink of my reverie. My focus snapped to his knowing smirk, his eyes glinting with the mischief of a man who knew too well the signs of a friend enthralled.

The abruptness of Killian's voice was like a cold splash, snapping me back to the present, away from the enigmatic siren who had commandeered my attention. "Austin," he said with that hint of impatience I knew all too well, "you gonna order some food?"

I shook my head as if clearing the fog of daydreams and turned toward the waitress. She stood by our table with an air of practised patience, her pen poised over a notepad, eyes expectantly fixed on me. As I observed her, my gaze fell upon the faint smear of ketchup on her apron, a silent marker of her labour. Despite its tired nature, her smile radiated an allure that echoed the innate grace of the woman who had captured my thoughts.

"Uh, yeah, sorry about that," I stammered, feeling foolish for being so easily derailed from the mundane task of ordering a meal.

"Steak and salad, thanks...and a coke." The words spilt out in a rush, and my gaze inadvertently drifted back to the object of my reverie. I could almost feel the warmth of her presence, the silent melody of her movements as if she were the sun, and I was caught in her orbit, unable to resist the gravitational pull.

As the waitress jotted down my hurriedly picked choices, I was caught in a whirlwind of unfamiliar emotions. There I was, Austin Carter, the guy who lived by the strict regimen of workouts and discipline, completely thrown off by a stranger - a woman who seemed to be cut from a cloth of an existence I hadn't quite figured out yet. Her elegance was like some silent poem that whispered tales of riches and adventures far removed from my college dorm life and sports turf familiarity.

Once the waitress slipped away, her footfalls fading into the restaurant's ambient noise, I sighed.

Killian's gaze flickered with mischief as he leaned back in his chair, eyeing me like a coach does a player who missed an easy shot. "Since when do you cougar chase?" His words danced around the table, teasing and light, yet they struck a chord deep within my chest.

I could feel the heat rising to my cheeks, that all-too-familiar competitive edge sharpening. "I don't," I shot back, more forcefully than intended. The image of her lingered at the edge of my thoughts. "But something about that woman makes me wish I did." It was true; she stirred a curiosity in me that went beyond the physical. She was like the uncharted territory on a map, promising adventure and discovery.

Killian's chuckle was a low rumble that usually preceded a bout of friendly ribbing after a well-played game. Beside him, Matt piped up, his voice carrying over the din of restaurant noise. "I can see the allure - she'd probably have some experience under that hood." He gestured vaguely across the room, but I didn't need to follow the direction of his hand; her image was seared into my mind.

A sudden, possessive tightness gripped my heart—a feeling utterly foreign and unsettling. "No!" The word burst forth, sharper and louder than I intended. Around us, the restaurant clatter seemed to pause before resuming its rhythm, unconcerned. Their warm and knowing laughter wrapped around me as they returned to their banter, assuring me with grins, "She's all yours, mate."

The adrenaline in my veins pounded a drumbeat, a wild soundtrack for the sudden surge of emotions that swept over me. Right there, smack in the middle of my buddies' wisecracks and laughs, I felt like I was standing on the edge of something massive. Part of me realised this wasn't about showing off or winning some stupid bet; it was about being drawn to something new, something tantalisingly out of reach - seasoned with wisdom and foreign experiences.

4

___

Piper

The encounter with the young athlete had left my heart fluttering in a way I hadn't experienced in years. After dinner, I felt an overwhelming need to escape before I made a fool of myself by approaching him.

Leaving the restaurant, I wandered through the resort, letting the tropical night air cool my flushed cheeks. Feeling restless, I explored one of the resort's many bars. I settled on one alive with the sound of island music and the scent of exotic flowers mingling with the sea breeze. The bar was a vibrant mix of colourful lights, tropical drinks, and infectious rhythms, making it impossible to stand still.

I found a seat at the bar, ordering a Mai Tai and letting myself be swept away by the vacation bubble. The music seemed to flow through me, and I swayed to the beat, the stress and constraints of my everyday life melting away. I wasn't twenty anymore, but I wasn't fifty either, and tonight, I felt young and alive, ready to embrace the moment.

I sipped my drink, savouring the sweet, tangy flavours, and relaxed completely. I was vaguely aware of the people around me. Still, mostly, I was lost in the music and the atmosphere, letting myself be carried away. I started to feel self-conscious when the feeling of being watched became too intense to ignore.

Trying to be nonchalant, I turned slightly, pretending to search for something in my bag that was draped over the bar chair. As I glanced up, my eyes met the same mesmerising blue ones from earlier.

For a moment, everything else faded away. The bar's noise, the music, and vibrant colours seemed to dim as I locked myself in a silent conversation with him. His gaze was intense and curious, and it felt like we were the only two people in the world. My heart skipped a beat, and I could feel the heat rising to my cheeks. Realising I was staring, I quickly turned around, breaking the spell.

I took a deep breath, trying to steady myself. The moment I had left me feeling exhilarated and slightly dizzy. I took another sip of my drink, attempting to compose myself. The young man was at the same bar, and I couldn't deny my magnetic pull towards him. But I also knew I needed to tread carefully. I was here to relax, enjoy my time, and not get swept up in something I wasn't unprepared for.

Yet, despite my best intentions, I couldn't help but feel a spark of excitement rolling through me. As I turned back to the bar, the image of him lingered in my mind, refusing to be dismissed. His intense blue eyes and the quiet confidence he exuded had left an indelible mark.

A part of me ached for the thrill of another adventure with a man, the kind of passion that had been absent from my life for far too long. But the rational part of me wrestled with the appropriateness of such thoughts. He seemed considerably younger than me, and the idea of pursuing anything with him felt like it might be frowned upon.

Yet, even as I tried to push the thoughts away, the prospect of being with him ignited a fire deep inside me. He was beautiful, obviously an athlete, and probably had the charm to match his looks. But I hadn't even been on the island for twenty-four hours. My vacation had just begun, and I reminded myself of why I came to Oahu in the first place – relaxation, self-discovery, and a break from my routine. Passion wasn't supposed to be part of the plan.

I took a deep breath and tried to focus on the present moment. The music, the warm tropical air, the taste of the Mai Tai – these were the things I came here to enjoy. Not to get swept up in the magnetic pull of a stranger.

The bar around me was alive with laughter and conversation. Couples danced, friends toasted to the night, and the vibrant energy of the place was infectious. I reminded myself that this trip was about me, about rediscovering my joy and letting go of the stress accumulated over the past years.

Still, I couldn't thoroughly shake the memory of those blue eyes. Occasionally, I glanced around the bar, half-expecting to see him watching me again. But he was nowhere to be seen.

With a determined sigh, I finished my drink and set the glass down firmly on the bar. I needed to focus on myself and the reasons I came here. I deserved this time to relax and enjoy my company without the distraction of a potential romance, especially one that seemed complicated from the start.

I ordered another drink and let the music carry me away once more, swaying to the rhythm and allowing myself to be fully present in the moment. Tomorrow was a new day, full of possibilities and adventures yet to be discovered. And for now, I was content to let the night unfold as it would, without any expectations or distractions.

But even as I danced and laughed with newfound friends, a small part of me couldn't help but wonder if our paths would cross again. And if they did, what kind of adventure it might lead to?

Austin

"JESUS H. CHRIST," I THOUGHT TO MYSELF AS THE WOMAN from the airport appeared at the resort right next to our training camp and in the same bar we ended up in. It felt like a sign, an almost uncanny coincidence that made my heart race with an excitement I'd never experienced before. The draw I felt towards her was magnetic, impossible to ignore, and only intensified my desire to be near her.

As I watched her search for something in her bag, I felt

like a starving man. Every movement she made was graceful and captivating. And then, all too quickly, she looked up, and our eyes locked. At that moment, the world around us seemed to fade away, leaving just the two of us in an unspoken connection that felt deep and undeniable.

I knew, felt it in my gut, that I was in trouble. I wanted to smile, break the orbit we were caught in, and show her I was friendly and approachable. Still, before I could muster the courage, she lowered her gaze and turned away. The moment was gone, and I felt a pang of disappointment.

"Stupid idiot," I chastised myself. Of course, my thoughts were just a pipe dream. This woman was way out of my league. She was older, sophisticated, and exuded a kind of elegance that I could only admire from a distance. What could a guy like me, a college senior still figuring out life, offer someone like her?

I leaned back in my chair, trying to focus on the laughter and chatter of my friends, but my mind kept drifting back to her. The intensity of our brief connection lingered, making it hard to concentrate on anything else. I stole another glance in her direction, but she seemed engrossed in the music and her drink, swaying slightly to the rhythm.

Killian nudged me, breaking my reverie. "Hey, man, you okay? You seem a bit distracted." I forced a smile, trying to shake off the lingering tension. "Yeah, just thinking about tomorrow's training session."

Matt laughed, clapping me on the back. "Don't worry, Austin. We'll crush it. But for now, let's enjoy the night. We're in Hawaii, baby!" I nodded, trying to let their enthusiasm pull me back into the moment.

But as the night wore on, I couldn't shake the feeling that my path and hers were somehow intertwined. Whether it was fate, coincidence, or just a simple crush, I knew one thing for sure: I wouldn't let this chance slip away without at least trying to see where it could lead.

Tomorrow was a new day, and I was determined to find a way to talk to her, to see if that spark I felt was real. But for now, I would enjoy the night with my friends, holding on to the hope that this adventure had only just begun.

Later that night, Killian, Matt, and I moved on to one of the resort's clubs. The lights pulsed to the beat of the music, casting vibrant colours across the room. The energy was electric, and I could feel the bass thrumming in my chest as we found a spot amidst the crowd and ordered drinks. We laughed, talked about our summer plans, and soaked in the atmosphere when I saw her again. She was with a group of people, and her laughter carried across the room like a melody that drew me in. Her presence was magnetic, and I watched her, captivated by every movement.

"Isn't that the same woman from the bar?" Killian asked, noticing where my gaze had landed. "Yeah," I replied, not taking my eyes off her. "This has to be a sign, right?" Matt grinned and nudged me. "All good things come in threes, Austin. You've got to go talk to her."

My heart pounded in my chest, and I could feel nervous sweat forming at the back of my neck. Now or never, I thought. I couldn't let this opportunity slip away again. Taking a deep breath, I stood up and started approaching her. The music faded into the background as I focused solely on her. Each step took forever, my nerves intensifying with every second.

When I finally reached her, she was facing away, engrossed in conversation. I tapped her lightly on the shoulder, and she turned around, her bright eyes meeting mine. For a moment, I was speechless, lost in the depth of her gaze. "Hi," I managed to say, my voice shaky. "I'm Austin. We keep bumping into each other, and I figured it was about time I introduced myself."

She smiled a warm, genuine smile that made my heart skip a beat. "Hi, Austin. I'm Piper. Seems like fate, doesn't it?" I laughed, feeling a bit more at ease. "Yeah, it does. Can I buy you a drink?" "Sure," she said, and we went to the bar together.

As we talked, I found myself even more drawn to her. She was intelligent, funny, and easy to talk to, and I felt our connection growing stronger with each passing moment. The nervousness I had felt earlier melted away, replaced by excitement and possibility.

We spent the rest of the night talking, laughing, and dancing. It was as if the world had shrunk to just the two of us, and everything else faded into the background. When the night finally ended, I knew that meeting Piper was no coincidence. It was the beginning of something special, something I was eager to explore.

As we said goodnight, I couldn't help but anticipate the future. This summer was already shaping up to be unforgettable, and I had a feeling that Piper would be a big part of that.

5

Piper

I stretched out on my beach towel, feeling the sun's warmth seep into my skin. The rhythmic sound of waves crashing against the shore was hypnotic, almost enough to distract me from the thoughts swirling in my head. Almost.

I was drawn to the water, where Austin was effortlessly gliding on his surfboard. His movements were fluid and confident, and each wave conquered with a mesmerising grace. It was hard to believe he was so much younger than me. Last night, he had been a perfect icebreaker, leaving me curious about what could come next.

I wasn't looking for a man, let alone one so much younger. Yet, our conversation had flowed effortlessly. Austin seemed smart, intelligent, and wise beyond his years. He made me forget the age gap, making me feel like we were equals. It helped that I didn't feel like an old hag myself, even though the years had undoubtedly brought their share of challenges and wisdom.

But what did I want with Austin? Was it just a flirty friendship, something light and harmless, or was there potential for something more relentless and passionate? The thought of diving into a deeper relationship was both thrilling and terrifying.

I watched as Austin caught another wave, his laughter carried by the wind. My mind wandered back to the night before. We had talked about everything and nothing, losing track of time as the hours slipped by. There had been a moment when our eyes locked, and I felt a connection, a spark that was hard to ignore.

Still, doubts lingered. What if this was a fleeting attraction that would fizzle out as quickly as it started? I wasn't sure I was ready for the complications of a relationship with someone younger, especially someone who made me feel things I hadn't felt in years.

Austin paddled back to shore, his smile bright as he approached. He shook the water from his hair, looking every bit like the carefree surfer he was. As he got closer, my heart skipped a beat.

"Hey, Piper," he said, dropping his board onto the sand. "Enjoying the sun?"

"Yeah," I replied, trying to sound casual. "You looked great out there."

"Thanks," he said, his eyes locking onto mine. "I was hoping we could hang out again tonight. Maybe grab dinner or something?"

I hesitated, my mind racing. This was the moment of truth. Did I want to explore this connection further, take a chance on something that could be amazing, or did I let my fears hold me back?

"Sure," I heard myself say, a smile forming. "Dinner sounds great."

As Austin's face lit up, I felt excitement and trepidation. This was uncharted territory, but something told me it was worth exploring. Whatever happened, I knew I wouldn't regret taking this step. Life was too short for what-ifs, and maybe, just maybe, this would be the start of something extraordinary.

Austin

THE WAVES WERE PERFECT TODAY; THEY WERE JUST THE right height and power to challenge my skills without wiping me out. I glanced toward the shore as I rode the crest of yet another wave. There she was, Piper, lying on a sun lounge, the sun highlighting her in a way that made it hard to look away. I could still feel the electric energy from our conversation the night before.

I paddled back out, trying to focus, but my mind drifted back to her. Last night, I had been something else. Piper was unlike anyone I had ever met. She was intelligent and confident and had this incredible ability to draw me in. I knew an age gap existed, but it didn't matter when we talked.

As I caught another wave and rode it smoothly to shore, Killian clapped me on the back as I exited the water. "You're in over your head with a woman like Piper," he said with a laugh. "Do you even know what you're getting yourself into? She'll eat you alive, man."

I chuckled, trying to brush off his words. "We'll see," I replied, feeling excitement and challenge in my chest.

Waxing his board nearby, Matt said, "You seem hypnotised by her. Ever since you saw her, you've been on her web."

He had a point. I had only spent one evening with Piper, yet from the moment I saw her, I was drawn to her like a moth to a flame. Something about her pulled me in, and I was eager to stay put. She was intriguing, like a puzzle I wanted to solve, but more than that, she made me feel alive in a way I hadn't felt in a long time.

I looked back at Piper, who was now sitting up and adjusting her sunglasses. She caught me staring and waved. I waved back, feeling a goofy grin spread across my face.

"What's the deal with you two, anyway?" Matt asked, curiosity in his voice.

"We're just getting to know each other," I said, trying to sound nonchalant. "She's different, you know? And not just because she's older. There's something about her that just clicks with me."

Killian raised an eyebrow. "Just be careful. Women like Piper don't play games, and you could get hurt if you're not serious."

His words lingered as I made my way over to Piper. I knew he was right, but I couldn't shake the feeling that this was worth pursuing. As I approached, Piper smiled, her eyes sparkling with the same curiosity and interest I felt.

"Hey, Piper," I said, dropping my board onto the sand. "Enjoying the sun?"

"Yeah," she replied, her voice warm and inviting. "You looked great out there."

"Thanks," I said, feeling a surge of confidence. "I was hoping we could hang out again tonight. Maybe grab dinner or something?"

There was a brief hesitation in her eyes, but then she smiled and said, "Sure, dinner sounds great."

I didn't know the future but was ready to find out. Piper had drawn me into her world, and I was more than willing to explore where this path would lead. Whatever happened, I knew I wouldn't regret taking this step.

6

Piper

The fabric of the slimline dress clung to me like the shadows that played across my bedroom as I prepared for the evening. It was a modest piece, its hue as dark and unfathomable as the night sky above O'ahu. Still, in it, I felt a resurgence of youth—a whisper of the woman I used to be, mingled with the assurance of who I'd become. The hem kissed just below my knees, a respectful nod to propriety, while the cut flattered without revealing too much. My reflection in the mirror bore the hallmarks of time gently spent: eyes still bright and keen, yet circled with the wisdom of my thirty-five years.

Sighing softly, I turned from side to side, considering the Piper that stared back at me. Once, boldness would have dictated my choice of attire, cleavage displayed with the same audacity that marked my early illustrations— each line daring, unapologetic. But tonight, the 'girls' remained demurely undercover, an intentional decision that felt like a silent pact between me and the universe—a pact to seek more than the fleeting desire that once fuelled my younger self's fire.

A decade ago, the thought of capturing his gaze with a mere flash of skin would have been the strategy—a game of visual tag where I was always 'it'. But this wasn't about the chase or the conquest. This was about connection, about finding something that resonated deeper than lust, that spoke to the layers beneath the flesh.

"Let's see if there's more to you, Austin," I murmured to my reflection, a playful yet pensive smile curving my lips. "More than just a handsome face and a body that the gods could very well sculpt."

With a final glance at the dress's tasteful elegance, I accepted the challenge I had set for myself. I wanted to discern if the spark I felt was kindled by genuine rapport or simply stoked by the allure of a younger man's charm. I sought the substance over the spectacle tonight, yearning for dialogue that danced around deeper topics, laughter shared over shared secrets, and perhaps, if the stars aligned, a touch that promised tomorrow rather than just tonight.

The balmy O'ahu air caressed my bare shoulders as I strolled down the dimly lit path, my heels clicking rhythmically against the pavement. The scent of plumeria mingled with the salty tang of the ocean. This heady perfume seemed to whisper secrets of the island's soulful nights.

I paused momentarily, letting my gaze wander over the eclectic mix of tourists and locals that peppered the sidewalk. Couples walked hand in hand, their laughter spilling into the night; families gathered around the sizzling food carts, their faces alight with the simple joy of shared meals. This was life unabashed and unrestrained, a vivid tapestry woven from countless threads of human experience.

A flutter of anticipation threaded through me as I contemplated my thread, the choices that had brought me here—to this island, to this moment. Even if tonight with Austin was just a vacation fling or a one-night affair, I craved it. The thought of being desired by someone whose youth pulsed with an energy that seemed to promise endless possibilities sent a thrill down my spine.

"Life is meant to be lived," I whispered, a mantra to bolster my resolve. It had been too long since I had allowed myself to savour the sweet nectar of spontaneity to take those rare chances when they arose. With dead-lines and conference calls, my life had become a mono-chrome routine lacking the vibrant hues of passion and adventure.

As I continued my walk, the quaint little restaurant came into view, its windows aglow with warm light, inviting and cosy amidst the tropical evening. There was a charm about it, a sense of intimacy that echoed the yearning within me—a yearning for connection, for expe-riences that would make my heart race with nervous excitement.

"Live your life again," the inner voice urged, embold-ening my steps. And so, with the soft rustle of my black slimline dress whispering against my skin, I resolved to embrace the unknown, allow myself the freedom to be vulnerable, and be seen not just as a competent illustrator but as a woman alive with desires and dreams.

"Let's start living," I said, more to the universe than to myself, as I rounded the corner and approached the restaurant entrance. The door opened before me like a gateway to new beginnings.

The scent of salt and sizzling garlic greeted me as I walked through the door, its rustic charm starkly contrasting the sleek lines of the resort behind me. A warm breeze toyed with the hem of my dress, a reminder that this skin hadn't felt the thrill of pursuit in far too long. The thought spurred a rogue wave of anticipation, cresting with the notion of being close enough to Austin to catch the musk of his aftershave.

"Wouldn't mind a ride," I confessed to the universe. It had been an age since anyone had stirred the dormant coals of my desire, let alone fanned them into a blaze. My ex-husband's tepid attempts at passion had left much to be desired. I often found more satisfaction in solitude than in his obligatory embraces. But Austin, with his youth and vigour, might just have the strength to reignite those long-forgotten fires—though he'd likely leave me bedridden for days. And honestly? The prospect of nursing a backache with a 'Bridgerton' marathon didn't sound half-bad.

The hostess, recognising my name from the incessant calls to snag a last-minute reservation, ushered me to a cozy corner bathed in the golden glow of fairy lights strung haphazardly above.

Settling into the worn wooden chair, I smoothed my dress over my knees, careful not to betray my nervousness. This wasn't just about physical attraction; I craved connection, a meeting of minds and not just bodies. As I scanned the menu, each dish seemed to echo my longing for something substantial—a rich and spicy life beyond the blandness served up by my past.

"Hope you haven't been waiting long?" The voice, threaded with mirth and confidence, pulled me from my reverie.

I looked up to find Austin standing there, with all sun-kissed skin and effortless charisma. His eyes held mine, a clear, striking blue that promised depths worth exploring.

"Only a lifetime or two," I quipped, my voice steady despite my pulse quickening.

He chuckled, sliding into the seat across from me. "Well, I'm here now."

Austin

I had always thought of desire as a linear thing, a path tread by the young and reckless, chasing after those with the same unlined faces and unfettered spirits. I wasn't a player or a man whore like the rest of my friends or teammates, but I also wasn't a saint. My tastes ran simple, undemanding—until Piper.

As I eased myself into the chair across from her, the creak of the wooden seat seemed to echo the stretching of my boundaries. The air was thick with the salt of the ocean, mingling with the faint aroma of grilled seafood from the kitchen of the beachside restaurant. I could hear the distant laughter of families enjoying their lavish vacations, the clinking of glasses toasting to health and fortune. Yet, all of it faded into a dull hum next to Piper's presence.

"Why have I never pursued something like this before?" The question lingered in my mind as I watched her tuck a strand of dark brown hair behind her ear, her green eyes roaming the menu casually.

My heart raced, thumping against my ribcage with the ferocity of a sprinter lunging for the finish line. Adrenaline surged through me, more intense than the rush before a game, a primal response to her nearness that left butterflies cartwheeling in my stomach. This was new territory, a different kind of competition where the stakes were higher than any championship—this was the game of connection, of vulnerability.

"Is everything okay, Austin?" Piper's voice cut through my racing thoughts, melodic and tinged with a playful curiosity that made me realize I'd been staring.

"Uh, yeah," I stammered, trying to regain some semblance of the composure I prided myself on. "Everything's great. It's just..." I paused, searching for the right words to bridge the gap between us without revealing too much of the chaos she stirred within me.

"Sometimes you find yourself stepping into a new arena, and it takes a moment to get your bearings," I finished, hoping the sports analogy wouldn't seem too out of place.

She smiled, that warm yet mysterious smile that simultaneously seemed to hold secrets and promises. "I know what you mean. Life throws us curveballs when we think we've memorized the playbook."

The restaurant's dim lighting cast shadows that danced across Piper's face, adding a layer of mystique to her already intriguing features. I found my gaze tracing the contours of her body, draped in a simple black dress that clung to her like a second skin, leaving just enough to the imagination to drive a man wild. "You look... incredible," I managed, my voice betraying a hint of awe.

"Thank you, Austin." Her lips curled into a smile that reached those captivating green eyes, eyes that seemed to pull me deeper into her orbit.

I shifted uncomfortably, hyper-aware of the tension building in my lower abdomen. The fabric of my trousers felt constricting, almost painfully so, as an undeniable physical reaction to her presence made itself known. It was maddening, this primal urge that surged through my veins with a ferocity that rivalled the adrenaline of competition.

I leaned back, trying to adjust discreetly, but there was no relief. My mind raced, thoughts colliding with the intensity of a high-stakes game, each one more scandalous than the last. It wasn't just lust—though that certainly played its part—it was the allure of the unknown, the challenge of navigating uncharted territory with a woman who exuded self-assurance and poise.

Piper's slender fingers danced elegantly over the glossy menu surface, her gaze flitting across the listed delicacies as if browsing a culinary masterpieces gallery. "What are you in the mood for?" she asked without looking up, her voice carrying the subtlest hint of intrigue.

I glanced down at my menu, though I scarcely needed it. The choice was automatic, habitual—grilled chicken and salad. "This one," I replied, tapping the description with a decisiveness that belied the desire whirling within me.

She raised an eyebrow, a playful smile curling the

corners of her lips. "Very mature choice," Piper teased, her green eyes glinting with amusement.

I chuckled, the sound slightly strained as I struggled to keep the conversation light away from the burning need that tightened my muscles. "We stick to a pretty clean diet when training," I said, trying to mirror her levity. It was true; discipline was the cornerstone of my routine, yet sitting here with Piper, I felt anything but disciplined.

Her response was a soft hum of acknowledgement before she leaned in closer, bridging the scant distance between us. The intimate proximity sent a rush of warmth cascading through me, and suddenly, I was acutely aware of every breath and every beat of my heart.

The sweet scent of her perfume wafted toward me—a delicate blend that seemed to capture both the comforting richness of vanilla and the tender allure of roses. Was there a hint of something more exotic beneath those familiar notes? My senses strained to identify it, to memorise the signature essence of Piper.

"Tell me all about yourself," she murmured, her voice lower now, almost conspiratorial as if we were the only two people in the world privy to this moment.

Inhaling deeply, I let her fragrance fill me, lending me a measure of calm against the storm of arousal. I began to speak not just about sports and fitness but about my family, the weight of expectations I carried, and the constant pressure to excel. With each word, I peeled back a layer of myself, revealing the contours of my life to this woman whose mere presence seemed to demand authenticity.

As I spoke, Piper listened with rapt attention, her eyes

never wavering from mine, her expression of genuine interest. In this dance of dialogue, I wanted to uncover her truths just as much as I wished to share my own. And somewhere amidst the exchange of words and lingering glances, I sensed the beginning of a connection that transcended age or experience—a shared understanding that we were both searching for our place in a world that often moved too fast.

7

Piper

As we sat and enjoyed a nice dinner and great conversation, I glanced at Austin's handsome face and beautifully sculpted body more than once. The thoughts running through my head were turning to barely legal.

His ocean-blue eyes and perfectly chiselled jawline only added to his allure, and focusing on the conversation was becoming harder and harder. When we shared a dessert, the heat between us became almost palpable. Every time his hand brushed mine, or our eyes met, a spark of electricity passed between us. The closeness, casual touches, and intensity of our connection made it difficult to keep my thoughts and actions in check. If I didn't get a hold of myself, I knew I'd take Austin back to my hotel room.

After we finished dessert, Austin suggested a walk by

the beach. I agreed, thinking the cool night air might help me regain composure. We left the restaurant and went to the shore, the moonlight casting a soft glow over the sand and waves.

We walked in silence for a while, the only sounds being the gentle lapping of the waves and the distant hum of the resort. The beach was quiet, and the atmosphere felt almost magical. Still holding my hand in his, Austin turned to me and looked deep into my eyes.

His gaze was intense, threatening to pull the floor away from underneath me. "You are so beautiful," he said softly, pushing a loose strand of my hair behind my ear. His touch was gentle, almost reverent, sending a warm shiver down my spine.

The closeness between us was palpable, and I felt an overwhelming rush of emotions—excitement, nervousness, and an undeniable attraction. He held my gaze for what felt like an eternity. Before I could even react, his face drew closer.

I stood still, letting him lead as his mouth hovered mere inches from mine. I blinked, and in that instant, his lips found mine. The world around me exploded into fireworks, my senses on high alert and an array of butterflies escaping my tummy. The kiss was soft and tentative at first, but it quickly deepened as we both gave in to our overwhelming attraction.

His hands gently cupped my face, his fingers brushing against my skin with a tenderness that made my heart race even faster. I felt myself melting into him, my hands finding their way to his shoulders as I pulled him closer. Every nerve in my body seemed to come alive, the taste of him intoxicating and the warmth of his body pressing against mine grounding me in this magical moment.

The sound of the waves and the distant music from the resort faded into the background, leaving us in our world. When we finally pulled away, we were both breathless, our foreheads resting against each other. His eyes searched mine, and I could see the same mixture of amazement and exhilaration reflected in them.

"Wow," I whispered, unable to find any other words to capture my feelings adequately.

"Yeah," he replied softly, his voice filled with wonder. "That was...incredible." We stood there for a moment, letting the intensity of the kiss settle between us.

The connection we felt was undeniable, leaving me excited and slightly dazed. I knew then that I was ready to embrace whatever happened next. Austin smiled, his eyes twinkling with a mixture of joy and mischief.

"I think this will be one unforgettable summer, Piper." I smiled back, feeling a surge of excitement for the adventures that lay ahead.

"I think so too, Austin." Hand in hand, we began walking back towards the resort, the moonlight guiding us.

Austin

"Don't go back to the resort just yet," I said, my voice filled with anticipation and excitement.

Piper looked at me, her eyes reflecting the curiosity that matched my feelings. "What do you have in mind?" she asked, a playful smile tugging at her lips.

"I want to show you something," I replied, gently taking her hand. "Trust me?"

She didn't hesitate long before nodding. "Lead the way."

We walked hand in hand away from the resort, the sounds of the night surrounding us. The warm Hawaiian air was filled with the scent of tropical flowers and the distant hum of insects. We walked for about twenty minutes, moving deeper into what looked like a Hawaiian jungle. The path was narrow and overgrown, but I knew exactly where I was going.

Eventually, we stopped at a beautiful waterfall illuminated by the moon. The water cascaded down in a silvery sheet, creating a mist that shimmered in the moonlight. It was a hidden gem, a place of pure magic I had stumbled upon earlier during my exploratory runs. Piper gasped softly, her eyes wide with awe.

"This is incredible," she whispered, her voice filled with wonder.

"I'm glad you think so," I said, smiling. "Now, how about we make it even more unforgettable?" Her gaze turned to me, curiosity and excitement dancing in her eyes.

"What do you have in mind?"

"Let's take the plunge," I said, a mischievous grin spreading across my face. "Shed your dress, and we'll jump in."

She hesitated momentarily, but then, with a determined nod, she reached for the straps of her black dress. I watched, mesmerized, as she let it fall to the ground, revealing her in just her underwear. Her beauty was breathtaking, and I felt my heart race with anticipation.

I quickly shed my clothes, leaving only my boxers, and retook her hand. We made our way to the top of the waterfall, the sound of the rushing water growing louder with each step. The view from the top was even more spectacular, the pool below shimmering like a jewel in the moonlight.

"Ready?" I asked, looking into her eyes.

She nodded, a fearless smile on her face. "Ready."

Together, we took the plunge, jumping approximately four meters down. The fall was exhilarating, the wind rushing past us as we descended. We hit the water with a splash, the coolness starkly contrasting to the warm night air. When we resurfaced, I looked at Piper, her face excitedly glowing.

"That was amazing!" she exclaimed, her laughter echoing off the surrounding rocks. I swam closer, pulling her into my arms.

"I'm glad you liked it," I said softly, my heart pounding with more than just the adrenaline of the jump. Our bodies were close, the water creating a sensual caress as we moved. I could feel the intensity between us growing, the desire in her eyes mirroring my own. Without another word, I leaned in and kissed her, the taste of her lips even more intoxicating than before. Our bodies moulded together effortlessly, fitting as if they were made for each other.

The rush of desire I felt for Piper grew exponentially, if possible. Each kiss deepened, becoming more urgent and passionate. We found it hard to pull away from each other, our lips seeking each other repeatedly.

In the heat of the moment, I wondered if it was too

soon to take the next step. But before I could overthink it, Piper took charge. With a flicker of determination in her eyes, she discarded her bra, her gaze never leaving mine. I caught my breath, struck by her boldness and the raw attraction that surged between us.

The moonlight painted her skin with a soft glow, highlighting every curve and contour. My heart raced, anticipation mingling with a deepening connection that felt undeniable.

"Piper..." I murmured, my voice filled with both desire and reverence.

She smiled, a hint of mischief dancing in her eyes. "I want this, Austin," she whispered, her fingers tracing lightly over my chest. "I want us."

At that moment, any doubts or hesitations melted away. I reached for her, pulling her close once more. Our bodies pressed together, skin against skin, as we kissed with a newfound intensity. The night, they seemed to wrap around us, cocooning us in their magic as we explored each other with a hunger that matched the crashing of the waterfall beside us.

8

Piper

The world seemed to hush around us, the waterfall's roar a distant symphony to the intimacy unfurling in its mist. Austin's hands, firm yet gentle, guided us through the cool embrace of the water, his touch igniting a trail of warmth on my skin. We moved as if in a dance, our bodies synchronised with each stroke until the smooth, flat rocks at the edge of the cascade beckoned us closer.

I could feel every droplet that escaped from my saturated hair, trickling down like tiny messengers between my shoulder blades, whispering secrets of the deep. Our lips met with an urgency that reflected the untamed nature surrounding us. I surrendered to the rhythm of his kiss—ebbing and flowing with a tender ferocity that mirrored the falls themselves.

Beneath the surface, hidden from the prying eyes of the

world, I sensed Austin's body responding to our closeness, his arousal pressing into me with a promise of what was to come. The liquid cocoon of the lagoon held us, a witness to the burgeoning desire that pulsed between us, as palpable as the island's heartbeat.

"Beautiful, isn't it?" Austin murmured against my lips, his voice a velvet caress that made me shiver despite the balmy water. "Not just the falls, Piper. You. Here. With me."

I smiled into our kiss, feeling a glimmer of something beyond the physical connection—a recognition of the improbable journey that had led me here, intertwined with this man who embodied the vigour of youth and an unexpected depth that belied his years. As his dick grew harder between my legs, a tangible symbol of our mutual longing, I couldn't help but reflect on the paradoxes of life.

The solidity of granite greeted my spine with an unexpected gentleness as Austin, with a strength that spoke of his athlete's discipline, hoisted me from the buoyant embrace of the water onto the rock's broad expanse. The stone, worn smooth by eons of the waterfall's caresses, still held the warmth of the day's sun, contrasting the coolness of the lagoon. Sensitised by our heated exchanges, my back registered every contour of the rock beneath me; it was like lying upon the surface of some ancient, slumbering beast.

"Got you," he said, his voice a playful whisper against the roar of the cascade nearby. His hands, firm and sure from years of gripping sports equipment, now gripped me with a tenderness that was incongruity more exhilarating than any high-stakes game.

With grace belying his size, Austin ascended beside me, his body a vision of youthful power and determination. He positioned himself above me, an embodiment of poised control, ensuring that my legs remained submerged in the clear, swirling waters below—a symbolic reminder that we were not entirely removed from the world around us, but at this moment, floating in an otherworldly space that belonged only to us.

My gaze lifted to meet his, taking in the scattering of droplets on his sun-kissed shoulders, the way his blond hair clung to his forehead, and the blue of his eyes, which seemed to reflect both the moon and the ocean's depths. How he looked at me, with a hunger mirrored in my soul, made me feel like I had finally found a treasure more affluent than any family legacy.

"Is this okay?" he asked, his concern cutting through the symphony of nature around us.

"More than okay," I breathed out, my voice barely audible over the falls. It was the truth. Here, with Austin, the weight of expectations dissipated like mist in the sunlight. No wealth or status could compare to the currency of connection we shared in this secluded paradise, where the only thing that mattered was the intimacy blooming between us.

"Good," he replied, a smile curving his lips—the smile of a man who knew the thrill of victory but was discovering the subtler joys of whispered promises and stolen moments.

As he laid me down, my upper body emerged from the aquatic veil, and my skin kissed by the humid air; I felt anchored yet free. Austin's presence enveloped me, a protective canopy that promised new beginnings and uncharted territories of the heart. And beneath us, the rock, a silent witness to countless seasons and stories, now cradled our unfolding tale—one of passion, discovery, and the timeless dance of two souls converging amidst the relentless flow of life.

The cascade's murmur crescendoed around us as Austin's mouth descended to my breast, a tender conqueror claiming uncharted territory with every brush of his lips. I arched toward him, an involuntary tribute to the skilled caress of his hands as they traced a waterlogged path down my torso. With a deftness that spoke of both hunger and reverence, he sucked each peak into the warmth of his mouth, drawing out moans that mingled with the symphony of the falls.

Time seemed to pause, the world outside our secluded cove slipping away like sand through fingers as his hand snaked between us. His fingers found the edge of my soaked underwear, the last barrier to my heated core, and I shivered with anticipation. Through the wet fabric, he began circling my clit. This slow, deliberate motion escalated into a rhythm as natural and compelling as the tide itself.

"Does that feel good?" he whispered against my skin, his voice a low vibration that resonated within me, chasing away any lingering shadows of doubt.

"More than you know," I confessed, my breath hitching as pleasure bloomed and spread under his ministrations. It was a candid admission that acknowledged how deeply he affected me—physically and in ways that transcended the confluence of bodies.

My hands roamed through his hair, tangling in the blond strands glinted with water droplets, each a prism reflecting our shared heat. I trailed my fingers over the breadth of his shoulders, muscles honed by discipline and competition. Yet, now they flexed for a purpose far more intimate than any game. With every stroke, I marvelled at his touch's paradox of strength and gentleness, a duality that echoed the complexities within myself—a woman born to privilege but yearning for authenticity.

"Keep going," I urged, lost in the dual sensations that Austin was gifting to my clit and nipples, my voice a heady mixture of command and plea. Each flick of his finger, each pull of his lips, stoked a fire that threatened to consume all rational thought.

"Yes, ma'am," he murmured, his words laden with desire and something deeper, something that hinted at the connective threads weaving together our disparate lives.

Austin

SENSATION CREPT UP PIPER'S SPINE LIKE THE TIDE OVER golden sand, and my touch became the relentless push of the waves. I concentrated, the tips of my fingers pressing with a fervent urgency against her as if I were coaxing every shadow from her depths to the surface in a cascade of light. The water of the lagoon embraced us, a silent witness to our clandestine symphony, its gentle lapping against our skin a soft percussion to the crescendo building within her.

"Ah... Austin, I'm going to..." Piper's voice broke through the hush, her words becoming part of the night's humid breath. Her body, a sculpture of flesh and longing, tensed beneath my hands—every muscle tightening, reaching for the precipice. With my name falling from her lips like an invocation, it was as if she granted me a power I'd never known, an electric surge that connected us beyond the physical.

She unravelled then, her back arching gracefully, a bow pulled taut before releasing its arrow. Water droplets danced along her skin, tracing paths over the valleys and peaks of her body, and in the moonlight, they shimmered like tiny liquid stars. She embodied every secret wish whispered into the night—a vision of raw, unadulterated beauty that made my chest swell with emotion too big to name.

As her pleasure washed over her, I watched in awe. The languid waves of the lagoon whispered secrets as Piper's breath steadied, her chest rising and falling with a rhythm that beckoned me back from the edge of awe. Her lips, swollen with our shared fervour, found mine again—urgent, pleading for continuance in a dance we had only just begun. "Austin, I need more," she demanded, her voice a silken thread wrapping around my resolve.

How could I refuse? It was not simply lust that compelled me but the magnetic pull of her confidence, the allure of her independence shining through even in this vulnerability. She was a siren commanding the tides of my desire, and I was helpless to the call.

As she rose from the water, it clung like an envious lover, reluctant to release her from its embrace. The moonlight painted her in silver strokes as she extended her hands toward me, her touch the promise of every hidden dream I dared not voice. My body responded to her, a loyal subject to her will; my arousal was a testament to her effect on me—a rock-hard declaration of my yearning.

Her warm hand enveloped me, and the world narrowed down to the point of contact. A surge of pleasure shot through me, eliciting a moan that seemed to rise from the depths of my soul. I was laid bare before her, every pretence of control slipping away like the water droplets that now journeyed across her skin.

At that moment, suspended between the water and the stars, I was no longer just a college athlete bound by discipline and routine. With Piper, I discovered new facets of myself—a man capable of both strength and profound tenderness.

"More," she had said. And more was what I would give.

"You're huge, Austin," she whispered a husky melody that rumbled through the tropical night air. The affirmation was intoxicating; it was an ego stroke no man could ever grow tired of hearing. As her fingers danced provocatively over the strained fabric of my boxers, I felt every thread strain against the growing pressure.

"Fuck, Piper," I gasped as her hand slipped beneath the waistband, her touch igniting a fire in my veins. Her fingers were warm and knowing, wrapping around me with a confidence that left no room for doubt. The pressure built was delicious and almost painful; each stroke stoked the flames higher.

"Stand up," she commanded, and her words were laced

with an authority that beckoned me to obey. Every fibre of my being yearned to follow her lead, to submit to the desires that thrummed between us like a live wire. I rose from the water, feeling the cool night air kiss my heated skin, contrasting with the warmth radiating from her palm that still held me captive.

My heart raced as she leaned in close again, her lips brushing mine with a tenderness that belied the urgency of our encounter. "Let me taste you." It wasn't just a request—it was a need that matched the hunger clawing at my insides.

"Yes, Ma'am," I murmured, surrendering to the moment. The rules of the world outside this secluded lagoon didn't apply here. There were no coaches dictating drills—just the freedom to explore this connection that had blossomed unexpectedly under the Hawaiian moonlight.

As she drew near, I was reminded of all the reasons I'd ventured so far from home: to discover parts of myself not yet touched by the rigours of discipline, to taste the sweetness of life unrestrained by the boundaries of who I was supposed to be. With Piper's breath hot against my skin, I found a new sense of purpose—one that was entirely our own.

I towered above her, the heat from her mouth an intoxicating contradiction to the cool breeze dancing over my skin. Moonlight bathed Piper's form in a silvery glow, accentuating the droplets of water that laced her curves like jewels. My breath hitched as her lips enveloped me, her tongue an agile artist painting strokes of pleasure on my throbbing cock. With each rhythmic pull, she wielded control, anchoring me to the present with a firm grip at my base. I fought back a groan, not wanting this moment to end in premature surrender.

Your eagerness... it's flattering, but pace yourself, Austin, I thought. It was all too much, yet not enough. I said out loud, "If you keep that up, I'm going to cum," Her eyes flickered up, a knowing smirk on her lips as she paused, releasing me from her warm embrace. She shifted back, her body gliding against the smooth rock until she emerged entirely from the water's embrace. The way she spread her legs was an unspoken invitation, and my gaze followed the path up her thighs, tracing the water's journey back into our secluded lagoon.

"Then distract yourself," she commanded with a coy tilt of her head, "by eating me out."

"Fuck me," I exhaled, my heart pounding with a fervour that matched the crashing waves in the distance. Her candidness was like a siren call, pulling me closer. I waded through the shallow waters, each step toward her a promise of the sweet release we both craved. Dropping to my knees before her altar, I submerged myself in the essence of Piper—her scent mingled with the briny air, creating an aphrodisiac only nature could concoct.

The taste of her skin was like the lagoon itself—pristine and wild—and as my tongue danced over her folds, she became the melody to which my every sense attuned. Her soft moans filled the night, the sound more arousing than any symphony of pleasure I'd experienced in the sterile gymnasiums and echoing halls of my disciplined life. My fingers sought her clit, circling with precision.

"Thank you for this distraction, ma'am," I murmured between strokes of my tongue, watching her reaction with keen interest. Her body responded in kind whenever I uttered the word—a mystery unfolding beneath my very touch. Curiosity piqued, I asked, "Do you like that, *mummy*?"

Her climax took us both by surprise, a tempestuous wave that crashed over us with unrelenting force. As I drank in her sweetness, my mouth sealed around her opening, I realised I had found the ultimate victory—not in medals or accolades, but in the shared intimacy of this moment, under the watchful gaze of the stars.

In her uninhibited grace, Piper offered me more than just physical satisfaction; she presented a glimpse into a world where wealth and family legacy paled compared to the raw beauty of genuine human connection. In her arms, I discovered a place where I could strip away the expectations, and the pressures, and simply be—Austin Carter, the man, not the athlete. And I hungered for more.

9

Piper

Dear God, I thought while my inner walls were recuperating from the intense high Austin had just served me. With every sentence where Austin called me "ma'am," I felt my body tense with an unmistakable need for more. My senses responded to his word like a rogue bitch in heat. How he handled me most sensually surprised me in the best way possible, yet when he called me "ma'am," it seemed to trigger my primal instincts. I was ready to give him all of me.

His mouth moved like I was his last meal on earth. His hands roamed my body deliberately slowly, exploring every curve and contour. Each touch sent shivers down my spine, and I melted into him, surrendering to the overwhelming desire that coursed through me.

The sound of the waterfall faded into the background as the world narrowed to just the two of us. "Ma'am," he whispered against my skin, his breath hot and tantalising. The word ignited something deep within me, and I felt a rush of heat that left me dizzy with longing.

I couldn't help but respond to his touch, arching into him and letting out a soft moan. "Please," I whispered, my voice barely audible over my heart pounding. "Don't stop." Austin pulled back slightly, his intense blue eyes locking onto mine. "I won't," he promised, his voice filled with reverence and raw desire. Then, before I knew what was happening and was sure he didn't calculate that next move, the word "Mommy" left his lips.

That was my utmost trigger, which I didn't know about. The world around me ceased to exist and was replaced by fire radiating from my core to every fibre of my being. It burned relentlessly, and I welcomed it like a lifeline.

The unexpected term sent shockwaves through my body, igniting a intense and all-consuming desire. My breath hitched, and I felt a powerful surge of energy course through me. Every nerve ending was on fire, and I clung to him, needing him more than ever. Austin's eyes widened in surprise as if he realised the impact of his words. But instead of pulling away, he held me tighter, his desire evident in the way he intensified his tongue's assault on my clit.

I was left shaking and in disbelief at the extent of what had transpired here and now. I was very confident in my person and especially in my sexuality. Yet, the whirlwind called Austin, who had tipped my world on its axis over the last seventy-two hours, had exceeded my expectations entirely with a simple mere word.

Austin

Piper's climax unravelled something animalistic inside of me, and I couldn't hold back for not a second longer. I parted her quivering legs beneath me further; nothing was going to stop me.

I positioned my body between her trembling legs and lowered my torso so I was face-to-face with her. Piper's cheeks were still flushed, and a sheen of sweat pearled on her forehead, on which I rested mine.

I was consumed by this woman, intoxicated. Her maturity, experience, and sheer beauty held me captive, and I wondered if I could ever let go. But for now, I wanted her to feel everything of me as I wanted, needed, to feel everything of her.

"You're incredible," I whispered, my voice raw with emotion. The connection between us was electric, the air thick with unspoken desire. I could see the same need mirrored in her eyes, a depth of feeling that took my breath away. Our breaths mingled as I slowly lowered myself onto her, feeling the warmth of her skin against mine.

Every touch and every movement was deliberate and intense, a silent promise of our passion. I kissed her deeply, savouring the taste of her lips, the softness that belied the strength I knew she possessed.

I lined myself up, and I slowly entered Piper to the hilt. All the while, this vixen of a woman held my gaze, making me feel like I hung the damn moon. Her eyes glistened when my cock expanded her walls, her mouth parted, and the tiny sigh that left her lips made my head spin.

I've had good lays before, some better than others, but

fuck, Piper got my heart pumping to a different tune, she made the blood in my veins run hot like lava. She accommodated my dick like her body was made for mine and the way she felt sent shivers down my spine.

As I moved against her, I felt her body respond, arching to meet mine. The rhythm we found was natural, a dance as old as time. Her fingers dug into my shoulders, pulling me closer, and I could feel the tremors of her pleasure matching my own.

"Piper," I murmured against her lips, "I want you to feel everything." She responded with a soft moan, her eyes half-closed in ecstasy. The sound spurred me on, a symphony that played to the beat of my heart. I was lost in her, in how our bodies fit together so perfectly, and in how she made me feel more alive than I ever had before.

I pumped into her more vehemently, hitting her deep. I hitched one of her legs onto my shoulder and from the way her brows knit together I knew I was hitting her sweet spot.

"I love how wet you are for me," I whispered into her ear and I felt her squeeze me tight which purged a moan from me. Her eyes shot open, "I love the way you sound," she said, her voice trembling like her legs around me. We moved together in a perfect rhythm, our bodies attuned to each other's needs. I could feel the tension building, a crescendo of sensation that threatened to overwhelm me. Every touch, every kiss, every whispered word of encouragement drove us higher, closer to the edge.

At that moment, it was just the two of us, wrapped in a cocoon of passion and desire. The world outside ceased to exist, leaving only the heat of our connection and the fire that burned between us. As we reached the peak of our passion, I held her tighter, our bodies trembling with the force of our climax. The intensity of the moment was overwhelming, a wave of pleasure that crashed over us and left us breathless and spent.

We lay together in the aftermath, our bodies still entwined, our breaths slowly returning to normal. I looked into her eyes, seeing a reflection of my emotions – the awe, the wonder, the deep sense of connection we had found. "That was... incredible," I said, my voice filled with awe. She smiled, her eyes soft and filled with contentment. "It was," she agreed, her fingers tracing gentle patterns on my skin.

At that moment, I knew this was something special I wanted to hold onto. Piper had opened up a part of me that I didn't even know existed, and I was eager to explore it further to see where this journey would take us.

As the night gave way to dawn, we held each other close. The waterfall, the night, and the incredible connection we had found would forever be etched in our memories, a testament to the magic that could happen when two souls came together in perfect harmony.

10

Piper

The soft click of the door shutting behind me reverberated in the stillness of my room, a quiet punctuation to the symphony of the morning's escapades. Austin's hand had just slipped from mine, the warmth of his touch lingering like the afterglow of a setting sun. I leaned back against the wood, the excellent surface grounding me, as I watched him walk away down the corridor, his athletic form retreating yet imprinted on my memory.

Never in my wildest dreams had I envisioned spending a night like that—a night where the moonlight danced on our skin and the gentle lap of the lagoon waters serenaded us as we lay bare, entwined. The raw vulnerability of being naked under the stars with a man whose age didn't even span three decades was something I couldn't have fathomed—until Austin. Until now.

The air in my room felt different, charged with the electric remnants of a connection so profound it scared me. I drew in a deep breath, the salt-kissed breeze from the balcony wafting over me, carrying hibiscus and sea spray whispers. I closed my eyes, savouring the sensory collage —the brush of his fingers across my skin, the taste of his kiss salty and sweet, the sound of whispered confessions spilling freely between heartbeats.

But now that I had crossed that invisible line and tasted the forbidden fruit of youth, I wasn't sure I could ever return to the orchard of my peers. Men my age seemed like relics from another era, their touch devoid of the fire and fervour Austin ignited within me. He compensated for what he lacked in years with a passion that spoke directly to my soul. This intensity made me feel alive in ways I hadn't even known I was dormant.

My past relationships, with their comfortable routines and predictable conversations, paled compared to what I'd discovered in Austin's arms. This wasn't merely lust; it was a meeting of minds, a fusion of spirits—a kind of magic that didn't discriminate by numbers etched in time.

As I peeled off my clothes, heavy with the scent of our mingling, I allowed myself a moment to marvel at the journey life had taken me on. I was, standing in the threshold of self-discovery, on an island far from the world I knew. I had come to O'ahu seeking solace, perhaps an epiphany about my future, but instead, I found Austin—an unexpected chapter in my story, urging me to rethink every narrative I'd told myself about love, desire, and the essence of connection.

Water cascaded down my shoulders, rivulets running

over curves and valleys that had been explored so thoroughly under the moon's watchful eye. As the steam rose around me, mingling with the scent of plumeria from my body wash, I couldn't help but let my mind drift back to Austin. His hands were firm yet gentle, his laughter ringing in my ears like the most enchanting melodies.

The reflection staring back at me from the foggy glass was flushed, glowing—transformed. Who was this woman who craved the youthful vigour of a man like Austin? This newfound persona within me was someone I didn't recognise yet couldn't deny. I was one of those women now, a 'cougar' as they say, finding a sweet, forbidden pleasure in being called 'ma'am' and 'mummy'.

I turned off the water with a quiet click, the droplets still clinging to my skin like morning dew. Wrapping myself in a towel, I stood there, pondering the dizzying thrill that ran through me when Austin uttered those words. The way he looked up at me through those captivating blue eyes was liberating, filled with an earnest desire that seemed to know no bounds. Yet, here I was, questioning if it was right to savour this role that society deemed inappropriate for a woman of my standing.

Slipping into my nightgown, the fabric kissed my skin, whispering secrets only the night would know. The image of Austin, bound to my bed, flickered through my consciousness, an illicit fantasy that sent a shiver down my spine. He was calling out for me; his voice laced with desperation and adoration, the title 'mummy' slipping from his lips and settling into the air like sacred incantations.

I crawled into bed, every muscle in my body reminding me of our age difference. Where he was buoyant and brimming with energy, I bore the graceful, albeit heavy, elegance of maturity. My head found solace in the pillow's softness, my body sinking into the embrace of the mattress as I succumbed to the weariness that enveloped me.

In the quiet of my room, with the faint rustling of palm leaves outside the window, I grappled with the reality of what I had given myself permission to explore. Tethered between the intoxicating rush of new experiences and the comforting anchor of self-awareness, I realised that sometimes, to truly find your place in the world, you must dare to venture beyond the boundaries of what is known.

I closed my eyes, and the canvas of my mind painted itself with the vivid hues of daydreams. The gentle hiss of the distant waves lapping against the shore provided a soothing soundtrack to my reverie. This holiday, this escape from the monotony of pencilled lines and magazine deadlines, was shaping up to be the salve my soul hadn't known it craved.

The air in my room held the warmth of the sun that had just begun its accent and my skin still felt the phantom touch of the ocean breeze intermingled with Austin's caress. I had come to O'ahu seeking a brief respite, a chance to live audaciously, if only for a moment. Yet, here I was, living more authentically than I had in years—years marked by carefully curated professionalism and an unwavering focus on a career that demanded everything of me.

A smile tugged at the corners of my mouth as I envisioned the lagoon, our clandestine sanctuary where the boundaries of age and expectation dissolved into the night. With Austin, I discovered a fervour I had compartmentalised, tucked away amidst familial expectations and societal norms that whispered incessantly about what a woman in her mid-thirties should desire.

"Live a little," my mother had said with a nudge before I boarded the plane, her voice tinged with mischief. Little did she know the breadth of that 'little.' Here, nestled between luxury sheets in a room that cost more per night than I'd care to admit, I found myself peeling back layers of identity I'd donned like armour.

A gust of wind rattled the windowpanes, pulling me momentarily from the depths of introspection. It seemed even the island encouraged my contemplation, urging me to explore the uncharted territories of self. I had spent so long building a fortress of independence, fortifying walls with achievements and wealth, yet within the span of a moonlit night, a young man with eyes like the clear Hawaiian skies and a spirit as free as the rolling tides had coaxed those walls to crumble.

"Is this what it means to find one's place in the world?" I murmured to the silence, my voice barely above a whisper. Not a physical space, but a fleeting moment where every piece of the' you' puzzle fits seamlessly together. Perhaps it wasn't about the age inscribed on our birth certificates or the digits that padded our bank accounts; maybe it was about the connections that ignited our souls, the experiences that etched themselves into the very essence of our beings.

Austin

THE SUN BORE DOWN ON MY SHOULDERS LIKE A SPOTLIGHT, casting long shadows of me and my two companions across the undulating dunes. Heat radiated from the coarse sand beneath our feet as we shifted restlessly, awaiting Coach's whistle. I stood between Matt and Killian, my muscles tensing in preparation for the gruelling training.

"Alright, you guys know the drill," Coach barked, his voice cutting through the salty ocean breeze. "Sprints to the flag and back. I want to see you push—no slacking!"

As the shrill sound pierced the air, we exploded forward, our feet slipping and sliding with each digging step. Running in the sand was like battling an invisible force, a million tiny grains conspiring to hold you back. But this resistance was what I craved—the burn in my calves, the pump of blood echoing through my veins.

Last night's memories flickered behind my eyelids with each blink—a cascade of moonlit skin and whispered promises. Piper's touch lingered on my body, a phantom sensation contrasting sharply with the abrasive granules now kicking up around my ankles. The tiredness that clung to my limbs was a badge of honour, each heavy breath a testament to the intensity of our connection. Yet, even as fatigue threatened to slow my pace, exhilaration propelled me forward. This exhaustion was self-imposed, a willing sacrifice at the altar of passion.

My heartbeat pounded in my ears, drowning out the sounds of the beach and the distant calls of seagulls overhead. With every stride, I felt the previous night weaving itself into my sinews, becoming part of the story my body told with each drop of sweat that beaded on my brow.

I ran harder, pushing beyond the physical demands,

driven by a desire to excel—not just for the sake of competition, but to prove to myself that I could balance the weight of this sudden, unexpected emotion with the discipline of my sporting life.

Sand flew in small, stinging clouds as Killian's stride matched mine, his lean form cutting through the humid morning air with an ease that belied the effort of our exertion. His voice cut through the rhythm of our footfalls, a casual prod into the territory I was suddenly keen to guard. "You didn't come back to the room last night, gonna spill?"

A bead of sweat trailed down my temple, mingling with the salt spray from our ocean drills. The question hung between us like the pregnant pause before a storm breaks, charged and expectant. For once, I found myself retreating behind a veil of secrecy, the previous night's memories with Piper too rich, too vivid to expose to the daylight scrutiny of locker room banter.

"Ah, we went out to dinner, then for a swim," I managed to say, my breath ragged from the sprint and the sudden tightness in my chest at the recall of her laughter echoing off the water, the moonlight painting her skin in strokes of silver and shadow.

Killian's smile was a slash of white against his tanned face, his eyes gleaming with unspoken challenge. "So did you get some? Are older women as experienced as they say?" There was a teasing lilt to his voice, but beneath it lay the genuine curiosity of youth, always hungering for the outline of the unknown.

The question seemed to hover in the thick, tropical air, and I could almost feel the weight of Piper's gaze, those piercing green eyes that promised depths untold. She was a siren's call wrapped in the guise of a woman who sketched dreams onto paper, a riddle I was content to leave unsolved.

"Let's just keep running, Killian," I replied, deflecting, my smile a guarded fortress as I picked up the pace.

Matt's laughter broke through the rhythm of our heavy breaths, a sharp sound against the gentle lapping of the waves. "C'mon, Austin, spill it," he panted, a mischievous glint in his eyes as he sidled up next to Killian and me. "I wanna know if I should be chasing older women..."

"None of your business," I shot back, my words clipped by exertion, heart pounding not just from the run but from the memory of last night—a secret I wasn't ready to share.

Killian's chuckle was carefree, almost musical. "Ohhh, it's like that, huh?" He nudged me with a sandy elbow. "You must like her if you're not gonna tell us anything."

Matt joined in, egging me on with a wide grin. "Or was it that horrible you don't want us to know the truth?"

A shake of my head was my only reply. I couldn't explain—the way Piper had unravelled me layer by layer, revealing parts of myself I hadn't known existed. It wasn't just about the thrill; it was the way she listened, how her laughter seemed to fill spaces inside me I hadn't realised were empty. The intimacy of her touch lingered on my skin, an indelible mark etched with tenderness and wild abandon.

The intensity of those feelings scared me. I instinctively picked up speed, pushing my legs harder, sand kicking up behind me, desperate to outpace the questions and the knowing smirks. Piper had ignited something within me that went beyond desire, beyond the rush of a summer fling. She had made me feel truly seen in ways that left me raw and exposed.

As the distance between my friends and me grew, so did the realisation that this was just a summer break, a brief interlude from reality. And Piper—she would soon be an ocean away, back to England, leaving me to grapple with the vestiges of a connection that had felt like the first true thing in a long time.

I didn't know how to articulate the ache of impending loss or the fear of what it meant to yearn for someone so deeply. These were uncharted waters, and I was adrift, navigating a sea of emotions that belonged to neither the sun-soaked shores of O'ahu nor the gilded halls of privilege I'd grown accustomed to.

So, I ran faster still, each stride a silent plea to the universe: Let me savour this feeling a little longer before it becomes just another echo in the corridors of my mind.

11

Piper

The late afternoon sun cast a warm glow through the curtains, gently waking me from my deep slumber. I stretched languidly, feeling a pleasant muscle ache from the passionate all-nighter with Austin by the waterfall. I should have felt exhausted, but instead, I felt oddly refreshed.

However, an unfamiliar yearning stirred within me—a yearning for Austin. The feeling unsettled me. I wasn't supposed to feel this way, especially not so soon and certainly not for someone much younger than me. I prided myself on being a stoic, mature, and classy woman. Yet, the immense need to be close to Austin was undeniable.

I allowed myself to indulge in the feeling for ten minutes, daydreaming about his touch, his smile, and how his eyes seemed to see right through me. Eventually, I peeled myself out of bed and dragged my body into the shower. As the warm water cascaded over my skin, my hands instinctively followed the path Austin had traced the night before.

Every spot he had touched ignited a memory, and an array of butterflies erupted in my stomach. I closed my eyes, feeling the heat rise again, desperately wanting to shake these feelings away and regain my composure. I finished my shower, wrapped myself in a plush towel, and entered the bedroom. I checked my phone, and there it was —a message from Austin. My heart skipped a beat as I opened it.

AUSTIN:

"I can't stop thinking about last night and how amazing you are. I can't wait to see you again."

I CHUCKLED SOFTLY, FEELING THOSE DAMN BUTTERFLIES flutter in my stomach once more. Despite my efforts to remain composed and detached, Austin had managed to break through my defences.

I dressed quickly, opting for a simple yet elegant sundress that hugged my curves in all the right places. As I moved around the room, I found myself glancing at my phone, hoping for another message from Austin. His words had ignited something within me, something I hadn't felt in a long time. Despite my reservations, I couldn't deny the connection we shared. It was intense, consuming, and utterly exhilarating.

As I stood in front of the mirror, applying a touch of

makeup, I realised that perhaps it was okay to let myself feel this way. Maybe, just maybe, it was time to embrace the unexpected and see where this journey with Austin would take me. With a final glance in the mirror, I grabbed my phone and headed out, my heart pounding with anticipation. The butterflies in my stomach were now a constant companion, reminding me of the passion and excitement that awaited me. And I felt truly alive for the first time in a long while.

Feeling restless and realising I hadn't eaten since last night, I headed to one of the smaller restaurants inside the resort to grab a light snack. It wasn't yet time for dinner, but my stomach made space next to the butterflies for something more palpable than love, air... and butterflies.

I found a cozy corner in the restaurant and sat down, ordering a chicken salad and a mint water. As I waited for my order, I couldn't help but replay the events of last night in my mind. Every touch, every kiss, every whispered word had been perfect. I shook my head slightly, trying to focus on the present, but the memories persisted. Just then, my phone buzzed on the table. I picked it up, and my heart skipped a beat when I saw Austin's name on the screen. I opened the message, anticipation tingling through me.

AUSTIN:

"Be at the south gate exit at 6 pm sharp. I can't wait to do this again, Mommy!"

A soft chuckle escaped my lips, and I felt a warm flush spread across my cheeks. His boldness and the way he called me "Mommy" sent another flurry of butterflies through my stomach. The intensity of my feelings for him was both thrilling and terrifying. I glanced at the time and realised I had a couple of hours before I needed to meet him. I took a deep breath, trying to steady my racing heart. Something about Austin made me feel alive, and as much as I tried to fight it, I couldn't deny the connection between us.

The waiter brought my chicken salad and mint water, and I thanked him with a polite smile. I took a bite of the salad, savouring the fresh flavours, but my mind was already drifting to what Austin might have planned for us next. A growing sense of excitement now accompanied the butterflies in my stomach. As I ate, I couldn't help but wonder what about Austin drew me to him so strongly. His confidence, intensity, and the way he looked at me like I was the only woman in the world combined to create a magnetic pull that I couldn't resist.

Finishing my meal, I sat back and sipped my mint water, my thoughts still swirling around Austin. Despite the age difference and my initial reservations, I was excited about what the evening might hold. Maybe it was time to let go of my worries and embrace the unexpected, to allow myself to be swept away by this passionate affair.

I glanced at my phone again, rereading Austin's message. A smile tugged at my lips as I imagined what he had planned. With a final sip of my drink, I stood up, feeling renewed excitement and readiness for whatever lay ahead. It was time to see where this adventure would take me.

I was eager and excited to spend another night with Austin, yet I caught myself more than once thinking about this new kink Austin had set free. "Mommy."

The kick I got out of it was unreal, and the mere thought of it sent shivers down my spine. My legs involuntarily rubbed together, a physical response to the intensity of my thoughts. This newfound desire both thrilled and unnerved me. I had never considered such a dynamic before, but now that it was out in the open, it consumed my thoughts. I needed time to sit down and explore how deep this new desire ran. Knowing myself, I knew that I would seize it to its fullest. As I returned to my room, I couldn't help but replay Austin's message in my mind. The boldness of his words, and the confidence he claimed me as "Mommy," all combined to create a whirlwind of emotions within me.

Austin

AS I PRESSED SEND ON MY LAST MESSAGE TO PIPER, MY heart began to race. The simple utterance of that one word had turned both our worlds upside down. "Mommy." Seeing where this new plot twist would lead us excited me to no end.

When I uttered that word yesterday, she responded in ways I had never witnessed before, and I was immediately hooked. I needed more. I needed her. Desperately. Yet, as much as my desire for Piper burned fiercely, I couldn't deny that something more than a physical connection drew me to her. Something about Piper held me captive, despite knowing her only briefly.

Her maturity, poise, and the way she carried herself with such grace fascinated me. But I knew I had to tread carefully. I was venturing into unfamiliar territory, and if I wasn't vigilant, I could easily lose myself in the depths of this connection. Piper had awakened something inside me, something primal and intense, and I found myself navigating uncharted waters with both excitement and caution. As I stared at my phone, waiting for Piper's response, I couldn't shake the anticipation of seeing her again. The thought of her smile, her touch, and how she looked at me quickened my pulse. I knew tonight would be another chance to explore this unexpected bond, to delve deeper into the magnetic pull between us.

With a deep breath, I reminded myself to stay grounded. Whatever this was between Piper and me was exhilarating and intoxicating, but it also demanded respect and careful navigation. I couldn't afford to rush into things, even though every fibre of my being longed to be close to her again.

I glanced at the time. It was nearly six pm, the meeting time at the south gate exit. Gathering my thoughts, I locked my phone and prepared to head out. Tonight held the promise of more moments with Piper. These moments had the potential to redefine everything I thought I knew about love and desire. Excited and nervous, I made my way to meet Piper, ready to see where this electrifying journey would take us.

Before I could gather my thoughts and head out the door, my phone pinged with a message. It was from Piper.

PIPER:

"Change of plans. Be my good boy and meet me at the Lagoon pool."

HER WORDS SENT A JOLT OF ANTICIPATION THROUGH ME, A mix of excitement and curiosity. The playful command in her message hinted at something thrilling that stirred a primal desire within me. I couldn't help but smile at her words and the invitation they implied. I quickly checked the time and realised I still had a few minutes before our meeting.

Despite the rush of excitement, I took a moment to compose myself. This unexpected twist in our plans only heightened my eagerness to see Piper again, to explore this new dynamic that had ignited between us. The walk to the Lagoon pool felt charged with anticipation. The resort's soft evening lights cast a serene glow over the pathways as I walked through the lush surroundings. Each step brought me closer to Piper and the mystery and allure she held.

When I arrived at the pool, Piper was already there, standing near the edge under the gentle illumination of underwater lights. She looked breathtaking, her presence commanding yet inviting. A rush of warmth spread through me as I approached her, my heart beating faster.

"Hey," I greeted her softly, unable to hide the smile

that tugged at my lips. Piper turned towards me, a playful smile curving her lips.

"Hey yourself," she replied, her voice hinting of mischief. "Glad you could make it." Her words filled me with a sense of excitement and anticipation.

"I wouldn't miss it for anything," I confessed sincerely, my gaze locked with hers. As Piper stepped closer, her hand brushing against my arm, a thrill shot through me at her touch.

"Good boy," she murmured, her voice low and intimate, sending a shiver down my spine. I felt a rush of desire, a longing to please her, to discover where this unexpected connection would lead. Her presence was intoxicating, her confidence and allure drawing me in deeper. I wanted to savour every moment with her, to explore the unspoken chemistry that crackled between us.

"I have something special planned for us tonight," she whispered, her warm breath teasing against my ear. My heart raced with anticipation, my mind racing with possibilities. I was captivated by her boldness, by the way she effortlessly commanded my attention.

"Lead the way," I replied, my voice filled with anticipation and a growing desire to see where this night would take us. With a knowing smile, Piper took my hand and led me towards a secluded corner of the Lagoon pool area. Each step felt charged with excitement and possibility, eager to discover what awaited us in the night's embrace.

12

Piper

In a last-minute effort, I booked the Lagoon pool to have it all to myself—well, for me and Austin. I had to pay extra, but for what I had in mind, I needed the area to be closed off and private. After last night's shenanigans and sitting down to hatch a plan, I concluded that no summer fling would be the real deal without pushing the boundaries. And by the looks of it, Austin and I had found our little treasure.

I took Austin's hand and led him to the cabana behind the main Lagoon pool. It was hidden amidst the palm trees, the perfect little escape within our tropical paradise. Inside, I had ordered some champagne and an assortment of fruits to be delivered. The cabana bed was simple but fit for purpose. I wasn't planning to spend the entire night out here, but to kick this new thing off, it was perfect.

Austin looked hesitant, perhaps feeling we wouldn't be

alone or would be found. I assured him he could trust me and that we had our place. He smiled at me, and I saw the tension in his shoulders ease. I didn't want to take things all the way tonight—not here—but that didn't mean we couldn't enjoy the pool, and its amenities, and have a little fun on top.

Austin shed his shirt and stood before me in just his swimming shorts. His eyes roamed over my body and my newly acquired two-piece swimsuit. It wasn't extremely revealing but left much to the imagination. By the way, Austin was looking at me, I knew I had chosen the right outfit.

"Wow," he breathed, his gaze locked on mine. "You look amazing."

A shiver of pleasure ran down my spine at his words. "Thank you," I replied, feeling a blush creep up my cheeks. "I wanted tonight to be special."

"You've succeeded," Austin said, his voice low and enthusiastic.

I smiled and stepped closer to him, feeling the electric tension between us. "Let's make the most of this," I whispered, taking his hand and leading him toward the pool.

We slipped into the cool water, the gentle waves lapping against our bodies as we moved toward the deeper end. The moonlight reflected off the surface, casting a magical glow around us. It felt like we were in our private paradise, far away from the rest of the world. As we floated in the water, I couldn't help but feel a sense of excitement and anticipation.

The night was ours, and I was eager to explore the boundaries of this newfound connection with Austin. The champagne and fruit waited for us in the cabana. Still, for now, I wanted to savour the moment, to let the magic of the night unfold naturally.

The water was cool against our skin, a refreshing contrast to the warm, humid air. We swam slowly, our movements synchronised as if we'd been doing this for years. There was an ease between us, a comfort that belied the short time we'd known each other. Every brush of his arm, every accidental touch, sent sparks of electricity through my body. We eventually found ourselves at the pool's far end, where the water was shallow and the trees formed a natural canopy above us.

The moonlight filtered through the leaves, casting dappled shadows on our faces. Austin turned to me, his eyes intense and filled with desire and curiosity.

"Piper," he murmured, his voice barely above a whisper. "This feels... different. Special."

I nodded, understanding exactly what he meant. "It does," I agreed. "I've never felt this way before."

He took my hand in his, his fingers intertwining with mine. "I want to explore this, with you," he said, his voice full of sincerity. "Whatever this is, wherever it leads."

My heart swelled at his words, and I felt a surge of affection for this young man who had so quickly become so important to me.

"I want that too, Austin," I whispered, squeezing his hand. "Let's see where this takes us. But first, let's have a little fun, shall we?!"

With that unspoken promise hanging in the air and my teasing, we drifted back towards the cabana, our bodies moving in unison. We climbed out of the pool and wrapped ourselves in the plush towels that had been provided. We settled onto the cabana bed, the cool night air drying our damp skin. I poured each a glass of champagne, and we toasted to the beginning of yet another exciting night ahead.

"Take off your shorts," I commanded Austin as we finished our drinks, in my most stoic voice. Austin's head shot up to look at me with surprise in his gaze. "Now, Austin!"

Taking this harsher yet promising tone with him was not even hard. The gentle wind caressing the palm trees outside, and the soft lapping of the water inside the pool were the only sounds to hear as the cabana fell eerily silent once my last words were spoken.

My expression was expressionless as I stared at Austin, waiting for him to undress. I easily slipped into my newfound role like it was meant for me. I dare to think maybe it was. And Austin would show me if this glove would fit. It took him a few seconds, but his face turned softer when the penny dropped for him.

He got off the bed, looked straight ahead and discarded his swimming trunks without a word. My breath silently hitched when he stood back up straight, and my eyes immediately went to his erection.

An erection he did not seem to have before I commanded him to strip naked in a stern voice. I had to take a deep breath before speaking my next words to not give away how much the sight of him affected me.

"Get on your knees, Austin." Again, he looked at me but this time his eyes not reflected any surprise though I did not miss the twitch of his cock. My body trembled on the inside, seeing Austin like this in front of me mixed with the excitement of my newfound kink.

He turned to stand right in front of me and dropped to his knees right before me without a word or even another look into my eyes. Once he was kneeling his eyes finally found mine again and I saw the fire of want flickering around his irises. His blue eyes were intense with unspoken need.

"Good boy," I uttered softly. "Touch yourself. Show me how good you can make yourself feel."

This was harder to say as my arousal ran through me like a freight train, but I needed to stay focused and see this through as it would bring me greater joy and pleasure than breaking out of my role would do. Austin's eyes grew wider at my request to show me something so personal.

He did not disappoint me though, his gaze went dark and a faint smile graced his precious lips when he grabbed his hard cock with one hand, not breaking eye contact with me. "Yes, ma'am." was his only response.

Austin

MY BLOOD WAS PUMPING THROUGH MY VEINS AT HIGH speed, I could feel the drum of my heartbeat throughout my body.

Piper just asked, no, commanded me to kneel in front of her and pleasure myself. I felt exposed but oh so turned on. Usually, I was not one to obey anyone. Yet, Piper's demands lured something deep inside me to the surface and I was ready and eager to obey her every command.

Her emerald green eyes looked at me with an intensity that spoke a thousand words. She was beckoning me to enter this new world with her.

As you wish, I thought.

Without breaking our eye contact I answered correctly, "Yes, ma'am." Then my hand found my painfully hard shaft. Piper's eyes wandered from mine to what she desired most.

I gave my cock a few slow pumps, the precum pooling at its head. Piper turned me on like no one's business, and my highest priority was to please and satisfy her needs.

She leaned back on the bed with her arms stretched behind her, holding her upper weight, her long dark cascading over her shoulders like a velvet robe, a small smirk tugging at her lips. It was a power position and I was at her mercy. She was watching me, her gaze following every stroke of my hand. I caught her licking her bottom lip, making my dick twitch.

It wanted to feel her warm lips wrapped around, her slick tongue lapping up every drop. My desire grew exponentially and I was unsure how long I'd last under her watchful eye. Though before I had to decide between stopping my strokes or cuming in front of Piper, her sweet voice brought me back.

"You are not about to cum, are you now?" My breaths came quickly, and it took me a few seconds to answer her.

"Am I not allowed?" She sat back up, her hands resting in her lap, maybe to stop her from reaching for me, but the calmness she oozed showed that she had fully under control and was not about to reach for me.

"Oh, sweet Austin, no you are not allowed." a chuckle in her voice. "Come here, lay between my legs."

With that, she scooted back on the bed and parted her legs. The panties of her swimsuit revealed nothing but I knew what was hiding beneath and I wanted nothing more than to bury my face there. Yet, it was not Piper's wish. With my back to her chest, I was lying between her thighs. She had one arm wrapped around my chest while her other slowly skated down to my cock. The moment she made contact I let out a low growl only for her to place one hand over my mouth.

My eyes shot up to her, but all I could see were her eyes fixed on her hand on my cock and a devilish grin gracing her mouth. I could have easily taken her hand that was holding my mouth close and overwhelmed her, physically I was her superior, yet I found myself still.

Piper started stroking my dick with gentle strokes, running her thumb over my sensitive tip lubricated by my precum. Her touch felt so good, her slow, shallow pumps teasing me. I closed my eyes and enjoyed Piper making me feel this good, when her pace picked so did her grip on my mouth. I didn't know what to do as that tingly feeling in my balls started, fire licking at my insides, jolts of electricity rushing through my veins. My hips bucked up and my back arched a little.

Piper let go of my mouth and pushed me back down into the cradle of her lap.

"Shhh," she cooed, wanting me to suppress what she made me feel. I was close now and ready to spill so I looked up at her, having an inkling of what I was supposed to do.

"I'm close," I said in a rugged voice, my tone hoarse from my swallowed groans, my lips dry from Piper's hand holding my mouth shut. As soon as my words were spoken she retracted her hand and my cock bounced to the side. The tingling, the fire and the electric jolts immediately seized me and left me with no room to breathe.

She was edging me and I did not know if I was built for this. The need to cum was so great, my head started to throb. Piper still wasn't looking at me, she was observing my erratic breathing. I didn't dare say another word, just letting it play out. When my breaths evened her hand wound around me once more, giving me a few soft pumps before she again picked up the pace and shot me up to the stars.

My climax was building inside me again, my back lifted off of her. "I'm close," a rather whimpery sound than my usual deep voice. Again, her hand retreated and my mind was ready to explode. God damn this woman!

I worshipped the ground she walked on. As much as this teasing drove me insane, I didn't want her to stop. The spiel was repeated four more times, and each time I barely made it to tell that I was about to cum. The fifth time she placed her hand around my throbbing and aching dick, her head lowered to my ear and she whispered, "You can come now, you've been so good."

Her words infiltrated my mind and made me so god damn hot that by her second hard pump, I exploded around her like I had never before. I moaned so loud and erratically that her other hand had a hard time covering my mouth and keeping me quiet.

I jerked up into her hand like my life depended on it and my sticky release covered my chest and dripped off of her hand. But Piper wasn't finished yet. She carried on stroking my spent cock to a point of pain. I writhed in her lap, whimpering with the ache she served me cold.

"Shhh," she whispered, pumping me faster. This post-orgasm torture set my brain on fire and I needed her to stop but at the same time, her dominance turned me on so much that I wanted her to keep going. Piper was damn near brutal and relentless, pushing me to my limits, exploring a hidden depth within me.

I never craved a woman as much as I craved Piper.

13

Piper

Austin and I spent the following ten days and nights together, and they were some of the most exhilarating days of my life. Our time was filled with passionate, boundary-pushing sex, opening Pandora's box more and more each day.

I wasn't used to what Austin brought out in me, but I welcomed it eagerly, pushing us both to our limits and beyond. I had developed this desire to dominate Austin, having him at my feet only for me to edge him to his absolute maximum. In return, he made the most passionate love to me. We complimented each other in every aspect. Despite our age difference and being both turned on by rather frowned-up on phrases.

When that man called me 'Mommy' I was done for. I never understood the appeal of a woman calling a man Daddy, but reverse these roles and oh my fucking God, I was ready to burst. He thrived on being dominated during sex and his stamina played well with my higher-than-average sex drive. When we weren't having sex he was however a proud man through and through, opening doors for me, having me walk on the right side next to him, pulling my chair out and despite being a college student he never let me pay for anything. It frustrated me but he insisted and told me to simply suck it up, he was the provider end of it.

During the days, Austin had to attend practice and participate in various activities that came with his program. But whenever he could, he would sneak away to meet me. Our time together wasn't just about sex; we got to know each other on a level that was entirely new to me.

We shared the same sense of humor and interests in sports, music, and movies. Our connection was deep and genuine. We went on proper dates like a couple at night, enjoying each other's company. We would laugh, talk, and simply be together, only to set each other on fire later with the most exhilarating intimacy.

I could tell I was starting to develop feelings for Austin, against my better judgment. More than once, I talked sternly with my reflection, trying to keep my head level and treat him like any other summer fling. But with each passing day, this became harder and harder.

I also sensed that Austin's feelings for me were intensifying. His eyes held a tenderness and longing that scared me. I couldn't let him fall for me. We were from two worlds across the ocean, separated by thirteen years.

I didn't want to get married again or have kids—something I never wanted to take away from him by loving me. We didn't speak about my departure, but I could sense the subject looming over our heads. He wanted to ask but hesitated, perhaps afraid of my answer. It hurt, but I knew it would be best to leave quietly, keeping him in my memories as the hottest and most affectionate summer I had ever experienced. Sitting alone one evening, watching the sunset from my balcony, I felt sad.

The thought of leaving Austin behind was almost unbearable, yet necessary. My heart ached at the thought, but I steeled myself. This was the right thing to do—for both of us. When Austin returned that night, we spent the evening wrapped in each other's arms, silent but connected. As we lay there, the weight of our impending separation was impossible to ignore.

The room was filled with a heavy silence, broken only by the soft sound of our breathing. I looked into Austin's eyes and could see the sadness there, a reflection of my feelings.

"I don't want this to end," Austin whispered, his voice trembling with emotion. I gently caressed his cheek, my heart aching at his vulnerability.

"I know, Austin. I don't want it to end either," I replied softly. He took a deep breath, his eyes searching mine.

"Piper, I've never felt this way before. What we have… it's more than just a fling to me. It's real." His words pierced my heart, and I felt a lump in my throat.

"Austin, I feel the same way. But we have to be realistic. Our lives are so different. I'm thirteen years older, and I don't want to take away your chance to have everything you deserve—marriage, kids, a future with someone who can give you all that." Austin's grip tightened around me, his eyes filled with determination.

"But what if what I want is you? What if none of that matters to me as much as being with you?" Tears welled in my eyes, and I struggled to keep composure.

"You say that now, but you might regret it in time. I can't bear the thought of holding you back or being the reason you miss out on those experiences." He shook his head, his jaw set with resolve.

"You're not holding me back. You're giving me something I never thought I'd find. You make me feel alive, Piper. You make me want to be a better man."

A tear slipped down my cheek, and I leaned in, pressing my forehead against his. "Austin, you're an incredible person. You have so much ahead of you. I don't want to be the one who dims your light."

He cupped my face in his hands, his thumbs gently wiping away my tears. "You could never dim my light. You're the one who makes it shine brighter."

My heart felt like it was breaking, torn between my love for him and our situation's reality.

"I don't know how to say goodbye to you," I whispered, my voice cracking with emotion. "Then don't," he replied, his voice equally choked. "Stay with me. We can figure it out together."

I closed my eyes, the pain of the decision tearing me apart. "Austin, I…" He silenced me with a tender kiss, and for a moment, the world melted away. When we finally pulled apart, he rested his forehead against mine, his breath warm on my skin.

"Just promise me one thing," he said softly. "Promise

me you won't forget this. Promise me you'll remember how much you mean to me, even if we can't be together." I nodded, my heart breaking with the weight of the promise.

"I promise," I whispered, my voice barely audible.

Austin

I WOKE IN THE MIDDLE OF THE NIGHT, MY ARMS WRAPPED around Piper like I was anchoring her to me. What she said sounded so final, and I felt my heart breaking for the first time. I wasn't lying when I said Piper made a better man out of me, a man she deserved. She was the woman I wanted. Despite the short time we had spent together, I knew an encounter like this would only happen once in a lifetime, and this was it for me. Piper was it for me.

With a heavy heart, I knew I had to let her go, as she had made up her mind, but not because of the reasons she gave me. She thought she was doing the right thing, sparing me from the complications of our age difference and different life stages. But she didn't understand how deeply I felt, how certain I was that we were meant to be together.

I sighed, tightening my embrace around her as she slept peacefully, unaware of my turmoil. All I could do now was hope and pray to whatever higher power existed that, if I was truly her soulmate, she would find her way back to me one day. Until then, I would hold a space in my soul for her, as I was sure she was mine.

I gently kissed her forehead, my heart aching with the

weight of the impending goodbye. I knew I had to cherish these last moments, to memorise the feel of her in my arms, the scent of her hair, the softness of her skin. I closed my eyes, willing myself to savour every second, to commit it all to memory.

"Please," I whispered, almost praying, "find your way back to me someday."

The night stretched on, and I held Piper close, trying to etch the feeling of our connection deep into my heart. Even if she left and we were apart, I knew she would always be a part of me.

As I lay there, holding Piper close, I felt a sudden surge of urgency. I couldn't let this night end without one more moment with her, one more memory to hold onto when she was gone. The thought of waking her filled me with excitement and sadness, but I knew I had to seize every precious second we had left.

I gently brushed a strand of hair from her face, my fingers lingering on her soft skin. Leaning in, I kissed her lips tenderly, hoping to rouse her from her slumber.

"Piper," I whispered, my voice filled with a yearning I couldn't suppress, "wake up, love." Piper stirred in my arms, and I pulled her closer to me, if that was even remotely possible. "You didn't think I'd let you go so easily now, did you?" I whispered into her ear, my free hand gliding from her perky tits down her belly to the sweet mound between her legs.

Piper shifted onto her back, still sleeping but her subconscious hyper-aware of me. My hand gently parted her thighs, and a soft moan escaped her mouth.

"That's my girl," I whispered again. She could sleep

the twelve hours on that fucking plane that was taking her away from me, but not now. Every second belonged to me. I let her dominate me during sex because it turned her on to no end, but that didn't mean I was incompetent in taking what I needed from her.

My fingers grazed over her heated centre, and she stirred once more as I dragged two fingers through her soft folds. "I need you wet and ready for me, and this time, I will tell *you* when you can cum and when not."

With this, I opened her and pushed my index finger against her clit making her back arch off the mattress. That's how I woke her up.

14

Piper

Austin's tongue was pushing me to the brink only to retreat every time I was ready to reach the precipice of my climax. I was squirming and writhing underneath him, begging him to let me fall.

"Please, Austin, for fuck sake. Please!" I whimpered. "How the tables have turned, beautiful," He teased back in between strokes of his tongue against my sensitive clit.

I was sure if he wouldn't let me cum soon my lower abdomen would combust. While he took his quick break to wait for me to come down from my near high, I started to plot my sweet revenge.

Dawn was nowhere to be seen yet and once I woke to Austin's fingers caressing my sweet spot I wanted to seize the morning with him.

When Austin was convinced I had come down he commenced his beautiful assault on my pussy. He slowly pushed two digits inside me, making me gasp; his tongue found my bundle of nerves and his other hand pushed down on my tummy.

With this combo, I was praying he'd let me cum this time, as it was past borderline torture now. However, I had little sympathy for him when thoughts of me edging him to breaking point crossed my mind.

My hands found the crown of his head, tugging at his blond hair, "Want something?" the arsehole asked mockingly.

"I'll leave now if you don't see this through!" I lied with gritted teeth, feeling the build-up of an orgasm cursing through my bones.

"Now, now," he replied to reprimand and curled his fingers inside me as he held me on a hook with no escape. My undoing was so close. With his curled fingertips Austin stroked me deep inside and I felt the slow contracting of my inner walls.

"Look at me, Piper." his voice was rough. I opened my eyes to find his gaze and he spoke with conviction when he finally said, "I want you to cum for me. Hard."

And that was all I needed to hear. Two more strokes of his fingers and I convulsed around them. My head tilted back, my eyes rolled into my head and I felt myself squeezing his finger tightly inside of me. His thumb found my clit and I let out a loud moan, fully immersed in the tidal wave of my climax. Only one thought went through my mind the minute the aftershocks left my body, and my wits returned. Revenge is mine.

* * *

I WAS KNEELING BETWEEN AUSTIN'S LEGS FOR WHAT FELT like hours. Kept edging him until his beautiful eyes started to water. My fingers had been wrapped around his cock for so long, and it wouldn't hurt to add my lips to the equation now, would it?

His voice was shaky, and his legs trembled when he begged, "Please, let me. God, please let me cum. Please!"

His words were pleading, but I sensed a touch of demand in there, too. I couldn't have that, not like this, not yet. I extended my arm, and my hand wrapped around his throat. Austin gasped in surprise, his eyes grew wide. His cock twitched eagerly in response and confirmed that he liked this.

He needed this as much as I did. Wanted it as much.

My fingers squeezed the sides of his throat tighter, not enough to cause him any harm, but enough for him to know who was in charge. I let my thumb glide over his sensitive tip and Austin let out this beautiful little whimper.

"You want to be a good boy, don't you?"

"Y-yes." He moaned. His voice was filled with arousal and torture simultaneously, and it was the hottest thing.

"Yes, what, Austin? You must be clear here, or this won't work, sugar!"

"I will be a good boy for you. Please let me cum, Mommy." And there it was. The resignation in his voice.

He was giving me absolute control over his pleasure. His eyes had been locked on my fingers around his throbbing cock, yet when he spoke the words, his gaze went to mine. I gave him a satisfied smirk in return and lowered my mouth, running my slick tongue along his tip before I took him in.

His back arched, a relieved whine escaped him, and his eyes rolled back. He knew I would reward him now for being my good boy. When he hit the back of my throat, I felt that he was not far off from falling off the highest edge.

Austin

I LOST ALL THAT BOUND ME TO REALITY ON MY LAST NIGHT with Piper.

I lay there, staring at the ceiling, my mind racing with thoughts and emotions. The last few hours I had just shared with Piper were mind-blowing. She had pushed me to new heights and limits, exploring desires I hadn't even known I had.

With her, I felt like there was nothing I wouldn't try or live out. Every moment with her was electric, every touch a spark that lit my soul. I could still feel the echoes of our passion reverberating through my body, a primal urge to keep her with me forever growing stronger with each passing second.

Yet, as I watched her sleep peacefully beside me, her face serene and beautiful in the soft morning light, a deep sadness settled in my chest. I would have to let her go in just a few more hours. The thought was almost unbearable.

I wanted to convince her to stay, to tell her that we could make it work, that our connection was too powerful to ignore. I even entertained a wild, desperate idea of abducting her, taking her away with me so we could live out this incredible passion without any constraints. But I knew better. Piper had her own life and reasons for leaving, and I had to respect her wishes.

No matter my intense feelings, I couldn't impose my desires on her. She needed to go back, and I had to let her. It was a bitter pill to swallow, but it was the right thing to do. I couldn't help but think about the future as I lay there.

One thing was certain: no matter how much time passed, I would never forget Piper and our extraordinary passion for each other. She had changed me in ways I couldn't fully comprehend yet and had awakened something inside me that I knew would stay with me forever. She was the woman who had shown me what it meant to truly feel alive, and for that, I will always be grateful.

I turned to look at her once more, memorising every detail of her face, every curve and line that made her uniquely Piper. I wanted to imprint this moment in my memory, to carry it with me as a reminder of what we had shared.

Leaning in, I gently kissed her forehead, my heart aching with the knowledge that this might be one of our last moments together.

"I'll never forget you, Piper," I whispered, my voice thick with emotion. "Thank you for everything." With a heavy heart, I settled back down beside her, holding her close as the reality of our impending separation loomed over us. I didn't know what the future held, but I knew that the time I had spent with Piper had been the most incredible experience of my life. And no matter what happened next, I would carry her memory with me, a bright, burning flame in the depths of my soul.

When Piper woke to get ready to leave, I didn't know what to do with myself. I felt out of place, like a stranger in my skin. Watching her move around the room, packing her things, every action seemed to accentuate the reality that she was leaving.

I could see Piper wrestling with her emotions, trying hard to stay calm and composed, yet her eyes betrayed her. Every time her gaze fell on me, they spoke different words —words of longing, regret, and a depth of feeling she tried to mask.

"You don't have to take me to the airport," she said, her voice steady but her eyes wavering.

"No one could stop me," I replied, a slight tremor in my voice. I had never been this emotionally attached to someone before, and the thought of giving her up now felt like tearing out a piece of my soul. She nodded, a small, sad smile on her lips, and continued packing. My heart ached with every item she put away, each a silent countdown to our separation. Piper didn't know that I had written a small note for her and stuffed it inside her suitcase, tucked away where she wouldn't find it until she unpacked her clothes back home.

It read, simply: "I'll be waiting for you." The note was my last hope, my way of telling her that this wasn't the end for me, that I was holding on to the possibility of a future together, no matter how slim the chances seemed.

I watched her zip up her suitcase, the finality of that sound echoing in the room and my heart. As we walked out to the car, every step felt heavy with the weight of impending loss. I couldn't bring myself to say much; words felt inadequate and hollow. The drive to the airport was filled with a comforting and suffocating silence, each of us lost in our thoughts and emotions.

At the terminal, I helped her with her luggage, our hands brushing occasionally, sending sparks through my body, a reminder of our shared connection. When it was finally time for her to go, I pulled her into a tight embrace, breathing in her scent, memorising the feel of her in my arms.

"I'll miss you," I whispered into her hair, my voice breaking.

She pulled back slightly, looking up at me with those captivating eyes. "Take care of yourself, Austin," she said softly, her hand lingering on my cheek.

"I will," I promised, my heart in my throat. "And you too."

With one last lingering kiss, she turned and walked away, disappearing into the throng of travellers. I stood there, watching until she was out of sight, a hollow ache settling in my chest.

As I drove back to the resort, the emptiness of the car mirrored the emptiness I felt inside. But the note I had left in her suitcase gave me a glimmer of hope. Maybe, just maybe, she would read it and realize that what we had was worth fighting for.

15

Piper
5 years later

The polished handle of my suitcase clicked into place with a satisfying snap, a small symphony to signify the commencement of a journey five years in the making. My fingers danced over the textured cover of my passport; the emblem embossed on its surface felt like a promise, a seal on a chapter yet to be written. With every intention set upon the American horizon, my heart constricted, an involuntary response as Austin's visage flickered through my consciousness—a cascade of memories that refused to be archived.

I manoeuvred through the bustling terminal, the air humming with the collective anticipation of travellers, each en route to their respective destinies. The scent of strong coffee mingled with the sterile chill of the airport, and I found solace in the familiar blend. America was calling, its siren song composed of dreams deferred and the magnetic pull of unresolved sentiments that tethered me to a time when my soul felt both shattered and whole within a heartbeat.

As I settled into the cushioned embrace of my seat on the aircraft, the soft thrum of the engines vibrated beneath my skin, a mechanical lullaby coaxing the plane aloft. Each mile between here and there stretched out as a tangible entity, an expanse I had once traversed with trepidation now approached with a boldness that surprised even myself.

Gone were the days when I allowed my life to be dictated by the whims of circumstance or the gravity of another's presence. Yet, amid the drastic transformations that propelled me forward, there remained a constant—a lingering ache, a silent whisper of what might have been with *him*.

Austin... his name alone was a vessel carrying echoes of laughter shared under a canopy of O'ahu palms, of earnest conversations etched into the backdrop of a setting sun. His absence marked the years, a silent calendar chronicled by the longing that crept into my quietest moments. Not once did I hear from him since our parting, not a single word to bridge the expanse of oceans and time between us.

And yet, I missed him. Every day since that fateful farewell, his absence was a note of dissonance in the melody of my life. It was a testament to the human heart's capacity for hope against odds, for nurturing a tendril of connection severed by both choice and chance.

Adjusting the strap of my seatbelt, a semblance of

security in the vast uncertainty that awaited, I let out a breath I hadn't realised I'd been holding. Life had unfolded in ways I could never have predicted, roads taken and untaken merging into the narrative of my existence. The changes I had embraced sculpted who I had become—an architect of my destiny, crafting a path lined with the stones of self-discovery and resilience.

It had been five years since I'd fled from O'ahu, five years since I'd felt the volcanic heat of Austin's touch, that seismic shift in my soul when our eyes met across the room. His absence was like a phantom limb, an ache that throbbed with every pulse.

I had returned to London, a city that once felt so familiar but is now strangely alien without him. The Thames continued its eternal flow, unconcerned with the turmoil mirrored in my chest. Love had been unexpected and fierce—like a gale that sweeps you off your feet, leaving you breathless and disoriented when it passes. Yet, in the wake of such a storm, I found a resilience I never knew I possessed.

In solitude, I discovered the art of conversation with my thoughts, learning to appreciate the silence that had once been filled with his laughter. I surrounded myself with the verdant tranquillity of the English countryside, trading the high-rise views for a cottage nestled amidst a patchwork of fields and wildflowers. There, enveloped by the gentle cadence of rural life, I recaptured a sense of self that the city had slowly eroded.

The cottage became a canvas for my rebirth, each brushstroke declaring independence. I painted the walls in hues of sunrise, a daily reminder that each dawn is a new beginning, a chance to sculpt the day into whatever shape I desired. Roses climbed the trellis, their petals unfurling like whispered promises of growth and renewal.

With the digital world at my fingertips, I wove pictures into stories from the seclusion of my sanctuary, my communication with the outside world tethered to the soft clack of keys and the screen's glow. And when the opportunity arose to contribute to an American publication—a thread pulling me back toward the land that harboured memories of Austin—I grasped it with tentative hope.

Engaging with the magazine was akin to dipping my toes into a stream, feeling the currents of a world that surged with vibrant life. Through articles and editorials, I connected with readers and kindred spirits who sought solace and inspiration in the written word. Each assignment was a bridge, spanning the distance between my quiet corner of England and the pulsating heart of American culture.

It began with one illustration, a daring and provocative piece that captured the essence of an emerging literary revolution. My fingers had danced across the canvas, imbuing it with shades and lines that spoke of feminine strength and sensuality for an author whose words set fire to the hushed whispers of women worldwide. That illustration became the beacon that caught the eye of the magazine.

I remember the email notification lighting up my screen, its subject line a siren call from across the Atlantic. I had read it, heart pounding, in the sun-dappled quiet of my cottage. In this place, I had painstakingly stitched together the fragments of my identity after leaving Austin's gravitational pull behind. The American magazine wanted me, Piper Robinson, to join their ranks. They were a titan in the publishing industry, their glossy pages a tapestry of culture, desire, and intellect that draped over coffee tables and filled bookshelves in countless homes.

With each article I penned from my remote sanctuary, I could feel the walls enclosing me stretch and dissolve, replaced by an expanse beyond the rolling English countryside. The assignments took me from the bustling markets of Marrakech to the serene temples of Kyoto, from the vibrant streets of Rio to the timeless ruins of Rome. With every stamp on my passport, the weight of what I had left behind in Hawaii lightened, giving way to an insatiable hunger for the new and undiscovered.

And now, five years since I'd breathed in the sweet, salty air of O'ahu and felt the crushing blow of parting from a love that was never meant to endure, I was ready to leap. Once a flickering flame, my wanderlust had roared into a bonfire, illuminating a path that led straight to the heart of Los Angeles. Here, amidst the city's sprawling dreamscape, I would carve out a space within the glossy pages of the magazine's LA headquarters.

I gazed out, lost in thought, tracing the outline of clouds through the window, reflecting on the immensity of change contained within the small confines of my suitcase.

Now, jet-lagged yet invigorated, I stood before the door of my new apartment nestled four blocks away from the pulsating heart of LA's creative district—a symphony of honking horns and distant sirens serenading my arrival. My fingers danced across the rough texture of the door before pushing it open, revealing a sparse space and echoing with possibility.

"Hello, new life," I whispered in my voice, a mix of trepidation and thrill. I felt the weight of the city's gaze upon me, curious about this newcomer, as I wandered through the rooms. Each bare wall is a canvas yet to be coloured, and every corner is a story waiting to unfold.

I sat cross-legged amidst the sea of boxes, rolling the term 'permanent position' around my tongue, tasting its foreignness. It was real—I was here, carving a niche in a place that didn't know me, where my reputation as an illustrator was just beginning to bud. Bittersweet, yes, but the sweetness lingered longer on the palate. I had left behind a love that once felt like it could consume me whole, understanding now that some ties must be severed to let new roots find soil.

"Here's to laying my stones," I toasted to an empty room, raising an imaginary glass. Outside, the city hummed, indifferent to the tiny victories and quiet revolutions within its midst. But I felt it—the electric charge of creation, the simmering excitement of untold narratives, and the undeniable pull of a destiny that was mine to shape, free from the shadows of restraint.

Austin

THE CROWD'S ROAR SURGED THROUGH MY VEINS AS I snatched my helmet from its hook, that familiar adrenaline rush tethering me to the moment. For four years, I had rocketed since I first laced up my cleats for a renowned LA football team, the dream of every gridiron warrior pulsing in the heart of America. The scent of fresh turf and electric anticipation mingled in the air as I ran onto the field, flanked by comrades-in-arms who shared the same relentless drive and the same hunger for glory.

Yet, as my cleats dug into the forgiving earth, a twinge of pain shot through my knee—a cruel reminder of the fragility beneath the armour, after three consecutive games on the sidelines, my once indomitable presence was reduced to a whisper among the field legends. My last season was upon me; the truth weighed heavily in my chest, an unwelcome shadow cast across my sunlit path.

The injury was a spectre that loomed, an uninvited guest at the feast of my career. The doctor's words echoed in my head with the clarity of a referee's whistle, slicing through the cacophony of cheers and chants—surgery loomed inevitable, and with it, the stark reality that I might never reclaim the full extent of my athletic prowess. The brilliance of my youth seemed dulled by the inexorable march of time, the edges of my future blurring into uncertainty.

Even as my hands adjusted the helmet over my head, securing protection, the fantastic plastic felt unfamiliar, almost foreign, as though acknowledging the change creeping into my bones. My gaze drifted across the stadium, the vibrant colours of the fans' attire blending into a kaleidoscope of dreams and aspirations, each one mirroring my quest for significance in this vast tapestry of competition and camaraderie.

"Stay sharp," I murmured, my voice grounding me.

The crowd's thrumming energy seeped into my skin, igniting the fire that had always propelled me forward. For now, I would play as if the spectre of my injury was just another opponent to outmanoeuvre, another challenge to overcome.

The crowd's roar faded to a distant echo as my cleats sank into the familiar turf, every blade of grass an old confidant whispering tales of past glories. The stadium lights cast long shadows that danced with the rhythm of my heartbeat, a syncopated reminder that change was not just coming; it had arrived.

With each breath, I embraced the duality of endings and beginnings, the bittersweet tang of transition lingering on my tongue. My future was inked onto paper now, a contract with the university that had shaped the contours of my ambition. I was ready to trade the adrenaline rush of the game for the steady pulse of a coach's life to mould young minds where mine had been honed.

In this arena of dreams, where I had once been the student, I was poised to become the mentor. The thought electrified me, sparking a thrill that rivalled any touchdown I'd ever scored. At 27, I was stepping back onto the soil that held the imprints of my cleats, ready to leave new marks, not as a player but as a guide.

As I stood there, letting the cheers of the present fold into the silence of my introspection, my thoughts drifted, unbidden, to Piper. Piper, with her dark hair that seemed to capture the essence of the night, her eyes a verdant mystery deeper than any playbook I'd studied, and five years had passed since O'ahu, since the serendipity of meeting her at a sports camp, since I'd recognised something in her that called to me like a siren's song.

The memory of her smile teased the edges of my consciousness, a phantom caress that could still ignite a fire within me. I had kept tabs on her from afar, a silent sentinel watching as she navigated her world with the grace of a woman who knew her worth. And despite her absence, despite the digital chasm between us, she remained etched beneath my skin, a permanent fixture in the landscape of my desires.

She had never responded to the note I left hidden amongst her belongings—the one that laid bare the truth of what she stirred in me. She believed our lives were meant to diverge, that I sought a future, she couldn't provide. But oh, how wrong she was.

I glanced up at the stands, searching for nothing in particular, yet everything all at once. It was time to play the game of my life, to chase down the elusive happiness that had slipped through my fingers once before. Watch out, Piper. This time, I refused to let go.

The stadium's roar enveloped me, a cacophony of cheers and jeers that pulsed through my veins like a second heartbeat. I had been angry, furiously so, when Piper had first left. I'd drowned the frustration in amber bottles and moonlit escapades, each hollow victory against faceless opponents leaving me more adrift.

In those restless nights, I chased shadows that bore her name—Piper. No one else slid beneath my armour, raking their memory across my consciousness with such sweet torment. I tried to replicate the feeling, dating women whose laughter echoed hers, whose touch I pretended could rival the inferno she ignited within me. Even older, more experienced partners left me cold, their sophistication no match for Piper's fiery independence.

So, I pivoted and channelled my wayward energy into the singular goal of becoming a gridiron legend. Focus became my mantra, and sweat and discipline became my companions as I clawed onto the roster of one of LA's most storied football teams. The limelight was blinding, the adoration intoxicating. Yet it was nothing but a gilded cage, its bars forged from expectations and prophesied destinies.

The high lasted until it didn't—until the realisation dawned like a California sunrise that I was a puppet dancing to someone else's tune. Then, I turned to the digital world, seeking solace in the pixels that painted her life. There she was—in London, her illustrations gracing the glossy pages of a prestigious magazine, her wit encapsulating captions that made readers pause and ponder. But not for long.

A shift occurred, seismic in its implications. Piper had traded Big Ben for the City of Angels, her talents now splashed across the magazine that arrived at my doorstep each month, a subscription I couldn't bring myself to cancel. A silent observer, I watched her world expand through the lens of social media—a move to LA, her new beginning mirroring my impending transition.

It was as though the universe conspired, aligning our stars once more. And there, amidst the thrum of anticipation and the scent of fresh-cut grass, I knew. The game ahead was merely a prelude to the pursuit that truly mattered. Piper's name was etched in the playbook of my future, and I was ready to execute the most critical play of my life.

My cleats dug into the earth, each blade of grass an individual beneath my feet as I took my place on the field, the crowd's roar enveloping me like a storm. There was a rhythm, a pulse to this life that had driven me, pushed me to greatness, and held me captive in its relentless grip. But today, it felt different because today wasn't about the game or the glory—it was about her, Piper.

I saw the glittering faces in my peripheral vision, a mosaic of anticipation. Yet, my mind was laser-focused on the future that awaited me beyond the stadium lights. My heart raced, not from the adrenaline of the sport but from the certainty that coursed through my veins. With every step I took across the turf, I inched closer to a destiny I had only dared to dream of—coaching, mentoring, and shaping young minds with the same fervour that had once consumed me.

And there, hidden within that future, was Piper—the woman who unwittingly became the compass of my existence, guiding me back to myself when I threatened to become lost in the tumultuous sea of expectations. In the silence between cheers, I could almost hear her laughter. This melody promised more than ephemeral joy—it promised home.

"Watch out, Piper," I murmured under my breath, a private vow made public by the intensity of my gaze scanning the anonymous sea of faces. "I'm ready for you now."

With a new job secured, my arguments were bullet-proof. How could she refute me when our paths were so clearly converging? When what I wanted—and needed—

was no longer a fleeting desire but a tangible, concrete plan that had her at its very core?

The whistle cut through the cacophony, signalling the start of the game. Still, it signified something far more significant for me at that moment. It was a starting shot for pursuing a shared future, where I could see us entwined in the mundane and the magical, growing old in a dance of giving and taking.

As I sprinted towards my position, muscles taut with purpose, I let my hand slice through the air, a wave carrying the weight of unspoken promises. The field stretched out before me, a temporary battleground that paled compared to the war I'd wage for her heart.

"Watch out, Piper," I thought again, the words a silent crescendo in my mind. "I'm coming to claim what was always mine." And in the depths of those green eyes,, I knew they were out there, somewhere; I hoped she felt the tremor of my resolve, as inevitable as the tide drawn to the shore.

16

Piper

I had acclimated to my new home and country with some bumps, but I seemed to get far well enough. Los Angeles offered an inexhaustible array of experiences, each more captivating than the last. The city's culinary landscape was far from what I was accustomed to, dominated by an abundance of fried fare and portion sizes that seemed intended for two.

Adjusting to this new norm posed its challenges. The climate of LA also invoked a certain nostalgia for London; the skies here lacked the mercurial drama I had grown to appreciate. Instead, an unrelenting warmth pervaded the atmosphere, filling my lungs with dry heat. Nonetheless, I enthusiastically embraced this new chapter, recognising it as an adventure too enticing to forgo.

My professional life flourished, with flexible hours and unparalleled artistic freedom—everything I had ever aspired to. Three weeks had passed since I awoke to an email from my employer detailing my next assignment.

My breath caught as I read the destination: O'ahu. Of all the places in the world, I was to return there, this time for business rather than leisure. The mere mention of the island's name sent a shiver through me, a blend of anticipation and trepidation.

O'ahu was my clandestine reverie, a chapter of my life I shared with no one, a treasure I guarded fiercely. I dreamt of Hawaii with regularity—vivid recollections of the waterfall I had visited with Austin and the intoxicating nights we shared.

These dreams filled my nights, a constant reminder of a connection that defied explanation. Rising from the bed, I moved to the bathroom, my thoughts drifting back to the resort where Austin had first asked me out.

My heart ached daily with the memory of him, but today, a different kind of fire stirred within me. Under the warm cascade of the shower, I felt an overwhelming need to reconnect with those memories. The water poured over me, and as my hands glided across my skin, I was transported back to the times Austin had touched me.

I could still feel the ghost of his fingers tracing my contours, his lips murmuring sweet nothings against my ear. The fervour of our nights, the way he made me feel cherished and alive, consumed my thoughts. Leaning against the cool tiles, I succumbed to the vivid recollections of our passionate encounters.

I knew I had to regain control, to centre myself on the present and the work awaiting me. The prospect of returning to O'ahu, the site of such profound emotional experiences, made maintaining my composure a formidable task. Taking a deep breath, I reminded myself that this journey was about my career, about capturing the island's inherent beauty through my lens.

Exiting the shower, I wrapped myself in a towel and gazed at my reflection in the mirror. The woman staring back at me was markedly different from the one who had departed London. I had evolved, learned to embrace new experiences, and confronted my fears with unwavering resolve. Yet, a part of me still yearned for the connection I had shared with Austin.

I couldn't afford to lose myself in these memories. I needed to be strong, to prove to myself that I could move forward without clinging to the past. But as I meticulously packed my bags for the journey ahead, I couldn't help but wonder if fate had more in store for me on the island that had irrevocably altered my life.

The weeks I spent in Los Angeles were transformative. I immersed myself in the vibrant culture, exploring galleries and street art, indulging in fusion cuisine, and savouring the endless summer.

The sun greeted me each morning with a warm embrace, starkly contrasting London's often gloomy skies. Yet, despite the city's allure, there was a void that only my memories of O'ahu seemed to fill.

My work has taken on new dimensions here, too. The creative freedom I enjoyed was unparalleled, allowing me to experiment and grow in ways I had never imagined. Yet, in quiet moments, my thoughts invariably drifted back to Austin.

Our time together had been a whirlwind of passion and

discovery, a chapter of my life that felt like a dream. The intensity of our connection had left an indelible mark on my soul. As I prepared for my assignment in O'ahu, I was acutely aware of the significance of this journey.

It was more than just a job; it was a pilgrimage to a place that profoundly shaped me. The island was imbued with memories, both beautiful and bittersweet. It was where I had experienced a love so intense that it defied logic and reason. It was where I had found a part of myself I hadn't known existed.

The anticipation of returning to O'ahu was both exhilarating and daunting. I knew revisiting those memories would stir emotions I had tried to keep at bay. Yet, a part of me longed to feel that connection again, to relive the magic of those moments with Austin. I wondered if he ever thought of me. Suppose he remembered our time together with the same fondness and longing.

As the departure day approached, I oscillated between excitement and apprehension. I was eager to embark on this new adventure, to capture the essence of O'ahu through my lenses and layouts.

Yet, I was also apprehensive about the emotions that awaited me. I knew that seeing the familiar sights, hearing the sounds of the island, and feeling the warm breeze on my skin would evoke powerful memories. On the morning of my departure, I took one last look around my Los Angeles apartment. It was a space that had become my sanctuary, filled with mementos of my journey and growth.

As I closed the door behind me, I felt nostalgia and anticipation. This trip to O'ahu allowed me to revisit my past and forge a new path. The flight to O'ahu was uneventful, yet my mind was a whirlwind of thoughts and emotions.

As the plane descended towards the island, I felt a familiar flutter in my chest. The lush green landscape, azure waters, and vibrant culture felt like a homecoming. Yet, beneath the surface, there was an undercurrent of longing, a yearning for the connection I had once shared with Austin.

Upon arrival, I was greeted by the warm, tropical air and the welcoming smiles of the locals. As I made my way to my hotel, I couldn't help but feel a sense of destiny. O'ahu had called me back, and I was ready to answer that call. I was here to work, create, and explore—but also to reconnect with a part I had left behind.

As I settled into my hotel room, I took a moment to reflect on the journey that had brought me here. From the bustling streets of London to the sun-soaked boulevards of Los Angeles, and now back to the enchanting island of O'ahu, my life had been a series of unexpected twists and turns. I had grown, I had learned, and I had loved.

And now, as I prepared to embark on this new chapter, I felt a sense of anticipation and hope. O'ahu was a place of magic and mystery, where dreams and reality intertwined. As I gazed at the horizon, I knew this journey was far from over. The island had more to reveal and teach, and I was ready to embrace whatever lay ahead. With a deep breath and a heart full of memories, I stepped into the future, ready to explore the depths of my soul and the beauty of O'ahu once more.

My hotel was conveniently situated not far from the resort where I had once stayed, and the pull of nostalgia was irresistible. I was compelled to revisit and take a stroll around its grounds. To my astonishment, the resort appeared precisely as I had left it five years prior, encapsulating a romance long consigned to memory.

As I wandered like a spectre through familiar haunts, scrutinising every visible corner of the resort, I noted that even some of the staff remained unchanged. My heart sank as I discerned the rowdy noises and sounds of whistles emanating from a nearby area—the athletic camp. It, too, was still in operation, with the unmistakable presence of college athletes.

The sensation of my heart being squeezed was palpable. I hastened my pace, eager to escape the memories those sounds evoked. I soon found myself at the entrance to a hiking path leading to the waterfall where Austin and I had shared some of our most passionate moments. Deciding swiftly, I followed the path.

Upon reaching the waterfall, a profound melancholy settled over me. Everything here had remained the same, a pristine nature reserve guarding one of my most treasured secrets. I circumnavigated the waterfall as much as the water permitted and settled on a nearby rock. Lost in reverie, I contemplated regrets, what-ifs, and an enduring longing that had haunted me over the past five years.

At forty, without a husband or children, I questioned whether my life had unfolded as it was meant to. Though I was content in many respects, there was an undeniable sense of something missing. I indulged my wistful fantasies about a life with Austin for a few moments before deliberately clearing my mind to focus on the mesmerising cascade of water.

The hypnotic sounds, the fresh scent of nature, and the sight of the waterfall brought back the intensity of those days we shared, moments that seemed both yesterday and an eternity ago. I allowed myself to imagine, if only briefly, what our lives might have been like had circumstances been different.

Would Austin and I have found a way to bridge the distance and differences that separated us? Would we have built a life filled with the same passion and love we discovered during those fleeting days? The questions were myriad, and the answers perpetually elusive. The continuous flow of the waterfall mirrored the persistent ache in my heart.

While I had moved on in many ways, the memories of Austin and our time together remained a poignant reminder of a love that might have been. Closing my eyes, I took a deep breath, allowing the symphony of nature to envelop me. For a fleeting moment, I entertained the fantasy that he might appear, that fate would reunite us at this very spot.

Austin

AS MY FINAL GAME CONCLUDED AND I FOUND MYSELF repeatedly at the doctor's office to ensure my injury was fully healed without the need for surgery, I had an idea that grew more exhilarating with each passing day. I had six weeks before starting my new position as a coach at LA's college football program, and my mind was consumed with thoughts of finding Piper again.

The island of O'ahu, which held my heart in a vice grip, seemed the perfect place to gather the last threads of strength I needed for this pursuit. After another visit with the occupational therapist, I returned home and received my clearance. I booked a trip to my favourite place.

In the past five years, I had visited Hawaii once, desperately trying to recapture the magic Piper and I once shared. And it worked. The island brought me a sense of calm, a solace I hoped would fuel my resolve and provide the confidence I needed to seek her out.

That evening, I met up with Matt and Killian, who, through a twist of fate, had landed on the same team as me. We gathered at our regular restaurant, a familiar haunt where the door personnel greeted me warmly and quickly ushered me to our usual table. Killian and Matt were already there, looking relaxed and content despite the gruelling game.

The conversation inevitably shifted to me and my new job as we discussed the match and their need for a massage after the ruthless tackles. We knew our bond was unbreakable, and I would no longer work alongside them.

And then, I dropped the bombshell: I had booked another trip to Hawaii. Silence fell over the table. With his intense gaze, Killian was the first to break it, asking if I would ever let it go. Would I ever let her go? Both had witnessed my yearning for Piper over the past five years, enduring countless conversations where they urged me to forget her. I knew they were tired of my relentless pursuit.

Matt shook his head, looking at me as if I had lost my

mind. But I wasn't deterred. A trip to Hawaii was set, followed by the start of my new position and, most importantly, finding Piper and making her mine. When I told them Piper had moved to LA, they initially believed I was delusional, thinking my imagination had finally taken over.

But I wasn't mad; I was merely attuned to the universe, bringing Piper into my path. I wouldn't miss my target again. The anticipation of seeing her again filled me with excitement and dread. I knew this journey was not just about finding Piper but about confronting the feelings that had grown stronger over the years. The island, with its serene beauty and the memories it held, would be the perfect backdrop for this mind-clearing I needed before I stalked her enough to cross paths again.

* * *

EMOTIONS OVERWHELMED ME AS I METICULOUSLY unpacked my suitcase in the serene confines of the O'ahu hotel room. Piper's presence felt almost tangible as if her spirit lingered in every corner of this island. Returning here, retracing our steps and revisiting our cherished places stirred nostalgia and determination.

Los Angeles, her new home, seemed simultaneously distant and intimately close. Realising that fate had led us to the same city after all these years felt like more than mere coincidence—it was a sign, a subtle nudge from the universe prompting me to seize this chance to reclaim what we once shared.

Carefully unpacking my belongings alongside my

thoughts, I ventured out to familiar spots that held remnants of our shared history. The sports camp where I was trained to be an elite athlete, the resort where our connection deepened—I wandered through these places with fond remembrance and unwavering resolve. Each location reverberated with memories oscillating between joyous recollection and a poignant ache of longing, reminding me vividly of a time when Piper and I were inseparable.

As the sun descended, casting a warm, fiery glow across the horizon, I found solace on the familiar beach where we once strolled hand in hand. The rhythmic crash of waves mirrored the ebb and flow of my emotions, stirring memories that had lain dormant yet were now vividly alive.

Sitting there, enveloped in the golden embrace of the setting sun, I allowed myself to reflect deeply on the journey of the past five years—how our paths had diverged. Yet, my feelings for Piper had remained steadfast and unwavering. In the fading light, a solemn promise emerged: tomorrow, I would make a pilgrimage to the waterfall, where our passion had cascaded freely and unreservedly. It would be a journey of rediscovery, a chance to reconnect with a pivotal moment in our shared history and perhaps find closure and renewal.

However, I lingered on the beach for now, breathing in the intoxicating island air that whispered tales of love and possibility. I was hopeful that Piper and I were destined to continue our journey together, wherever it might lead us next.

* * *

THE NEXT DAY WAS FILLED WITH VISITS AND OLD memories. First, I went to see my old coach at the camp. Five years had passed since our last meeting, but time hadn't seemed to touch him. He still exuded the same vigour and determination that had driven us young athletes to push our limits.

His eyes lit up with recognition and pride as he saw me. "Austin!" he bellowed, his voice echoing across the campgrounds. "Look at you! I've been following you, Killian, and Matt. I am sad about your injury but elated about your new coaching position. Maybe I should've been harder on you," he added with his infectious, booming laugh.

We spent the morning catching up and talking shop, reminiscing and discussing the future of the camp and its athletes. It felt like no time had passed, and the familiarity was comforting. After our conversation, I had lunch at the resort restaurant. I had booked my hotel room there again, seeking the closeness to the memories of Piper that this place held. The restaurant buzzed with life, but my mind was elsewhere, lost in the past.

Determined to revisit the waterfall, I went on the hiking trail that afternoon. Every step along the path triggered flashbacks of the times I had walked here with Piper. Each tree, each bend in the trail, held a memory. As I reached the clearing, the sight of the waterfall took my breath away again. The cascading water and the surrounding lush greenery were all just as I remembered, and they stirred something deep within me.

The waterfall instantly became my favourite spot when I discovered it, made infinitely more special by the intimate moments shared with Piper. I walked further out, taking in every detail. Someone was sitting on a rock on the other side, partially obscured by the falling water. The sound of the waterfall was hypnotising, and I contemplated taking a dip for old times' sake. As I shuck off my t-shirt and shoes, the person on the other side of the waterfall stood up and started making their way over. I turned back around, my heart nearly stopping as I recognised her. Piper. She moved through the water, her figure becoming more apparent with each step. My breath caught in my throat, a whirlwind of emotions crashing over me.

Five years had passed, but seeing her here, in this place with so much meaning, felt surreal. "Piper," I whispered, almost afraid to believe it was real. Her eyes met mine, and everything else faded away at that moment. The years apart, the distance, the uncertainty – none mattered anymore.

17

Piper

I had sketched its tale across his face, etching lines onto his forehead that hadn't been there five years ago when we parted. I stood motionless, my heart thudding as I observed him from afar. The breeze carried the scent of the waterfall to me, mingling with the intoxicating freshness of the surrounding greenery. Still, all my senses seemed tuned only to him. I'd made it a mission of mine not to check on him online, not to torture myself with the could-have-been. I had crafted an invisible shield, ensuring I didn't watch any sporting news to hear updates about his career, to keep him neatly tucked away in the corner of my mind where memories lay dormant.

But here he was, as if conjured by my deepest yearnings, standing in our secret haven. Seeing him in this alcove of nature that had been witness to whispered promises and tender caresses made me feel like I was walking towards a mirage. It was our spot—a place that transcended the ordinary, where time seemed to bend and curve around us, wrapping us in its eternal embrace.

He was beautiful—possessing the type of beauty that comes with young age, a vibrancy that pulsed beneath the surface of his skin. Yet, there was an aura of maturity about him that seemed well beyond his years, a wisdom that perhaps sprouted from the soil of trials we never faced together. His presence was a familiar and startlingly new paradox, beckoning me with a silent call that resonated deep within my bones.

I noted how his shoulders broadened since I last saw him and how his hair, once rebelliously tousled hair, now fell in a more controlled fashion. There was a quiet confidence in his stance, an unspoken understanding of life's capriciousness. And despite the changes, distance, and years that had woven their intricate patterns between us, the essence of who he was—the core of his being— remained untouched, untainted.

Water droplets clung to my skin like the remnants of a dream I wasn't ready to wake from. The waterfall's roar engulfed the silence, a symphony of nature that spoke directly to my soul. I moved with an ease of familiarity, my feet finding their way along the slick rocks that had been the silent witnesses to so many of our shared confidences.

Austin stood statuesque against the lush backdrop, his face a canvas of shock, mouth slightly agape as if he were trying to draw breath from the very surprise that held him captive. It was as though time itself had conspired to pause, granting us this interlude, this collision of past and present in a place that had nurtured the roots of our once entwined lives.

I felt the weight of his intense and unyielding gaze as I approached. Clad only in my bathing suit, I revealed in the liberating sensation of water dripping from my body, each rivulet a testament to the raw beauty of this hidden oasis— a place that had drawn me back, day after day since my arrival.

Despite the myriad paths I'd walked, lined with accolades and affirmations of a successful career, nothing matched the intoxicating rush of memories this place induced.

With each step closer to Austin, those memories grew more vivid, painting a mural of emotions on the canvas of my mind. Here, amidst the verdant embrace of nature, we were stripped of pretence, wealth, and the societal constructs that too often dictated our choices. Here, we were simply two souls reconnecting, perhaps for a reason, maybe just to remind ourselves of the journey we had once shared.

The waterfall's mist kissed my skin, a soothing balm to the heat of the Hawaiian sun and the simmering anticipation of what Austin's presence meant. As I reached where he stood, rooted in place, the world outside our cocoon disappeared. It was just us, the waterfall, and an unwritten future waiting to be seized.

The space between us dwindled to a mere whisper of air, and I halted just shy of arm's reach. Water droplets trickled from my saturated hair, tracing rivulets along the curve of my collarbone before succumbing to gravity's pull on the sun-warmed rocks below. His eyes—a tempestuous blend of ocean and sky—locked onto mine. For a heart-beat, I wondered if he recognised the woman I had become.

"I fancy meeting you here," I murmured, a soft siren calling over the waterfall's relentless roar.

Austin's lips parted, the ghost of his usually confident smile flickering at the edges. But no sound emerged. He stood there, as magnificent as I remembered, yet rendered mute by the moment. It was endearing, watching him grapple with the reality of me standing before him—a tableau of flesh and memory where once there had been only silence and longing.

His mouth moved again, a silent echo of unvoiced words, and my heart swelled. In that instant, he was not the charismatic athlete who could charm an entire stadium; he was simply Austin, vulnerable and beautifully human. The juxtaposition of his muscular frame, honed from years of discipline and sport, against this boyish display of aston-ishment made him all the more real.

I couldn't help but think how much like a fish he appeared, those full lips opening and closing in search of oxygen or perhaps searching for the right thing to say. A chuckle bubbled up from within me, spilling into the space between us, and I hoped it would coax him back to the present—to me.

Time stretched tautly, and we stood on the threshold of rediscovery. At the same time, the waterfall sang its age-old lullaby, inviting us to dive into whatever came next. I arched an eyebrow, leaned ever so slightly into the void between us, and repeated with a playful lilt, "I'm going to take the silence as a compliment."

Then, he seemed to shudder back to life, like a statue granted breath. His hand, warm and sure, reached out to me, brushing aside a stray tendril of my hair that clung to my damp cheek. "Piper," he began, his voice barely above a whisper, as if afraid to break the spell of the moment, "you're the most beautiful woman I've ever met."

His words, simple and sincere, wove around me like a warm breeze. I could feel a smile tugging at the corners of my lips, coaxing them into a wide grin as my skin flushed with a sudden rush of heat. My eyes darted down, shyly avoiding his gaze, focusing on the uneven terrain beneath our bare feet.

"Thank you, handsome," I murmured, the words tumbling out amidst a soft chuckle. The sound seemed too loud in the cathedral of nature we stood in, where the waterfall's cascade served as both barrier and bond, isolating us from the world beyond.

There, amidst the heady scent of wildflowers and the chorus of tropical birds, I stood at the crossroads of past and present. In Austin's blue eyes—a reflection of the sky above—I saw the boy who had once captured my heart and the man who held it now. It was as if all the wealth of experience and the longing for family and belonging coalesced in this one encounter, here in our spot, where the world shrunk to just the two of us.

His firm yet gentle fingers nudged my chin upward, compelling me to meet the ocean of his gaze once more. Austin's touch was a vivid reminder of our intertwined histories, the silent conversations we had held in glances, and the unspoken promises that lingered in the air like the haunting melody of an unfinished symphony.

"We played it your way for five years," he said, the timbre of his voice resonating with a gravitas that belied his years. It was a voice that spoke not only of the exuberance of youth but of a soul shaped by the relentless pursuit of personal excellence—a testament to the weight of legacy and the buoyancy of hope.

I could feel the whisper of his breath, its warmth sending ripples across the cool droplets left on my skin by the waterfall's embrace. His earnest and unwavering blue eyes anchored me in the present—a beacon cutting through the fog of my indecision.

"…Now it's time to play it my way," he continued, the corner of his mouth curling into a smile that held all the promise of a new chapter, one written in the ink of passion and the courage to leap into the unknown.

The world seemed to pause, the usual cacophony of nature hushed as if in reverence to the moment unfolding. The waterfall hummed a soft lullaby, the rocks beneath our feet solid and sure—silent witnesses to the seismic shift occurring in the fault lines of my guarded heart.

And then he leaned in, closing the distance between us with a kiss at once, a question and an answer—an essential turning in the long-locked door of my deepest desires. It was a kiss that spoke of family dinners yet to be shared, of wealth measured not in currency but in moments like this, and of finding one's place in a world that often seemed too vast to navigate alone.

As his lips met mine, I surrendered to the sensation, the taste of salt and sweetness mingling in a dance as ageless as time itself. In that kiss, I found the echoes of laughter, the shadows of tears, and the intertwining of our separate journeys that had led us, inexplicably and inevitably, back to each other.

Austin

The second our lips met, a wave of familiarity washed through me, flooding every corner of my being with the sense of returning to a place of warmth and light. It was as if I had been wandering for years, only to stumble upon the doorway to my sanctuary nestled within the softness of Piper's kiss. This was my sanctuary, refuge, and unequivocal happy place in the quiet lull of the Hawaiian sun. The thought swelled my heart with a potent emotion that threatened to spill over.

"Home," I murmured against her lips. The word was barely a whisper, but it encapsulated everything I felt then.

Piper's presence was a melody long ago imprinted itself on my soul. Now it played again, vibrant and beautiful. Five years had passed since she had walked away with those parting words that seemed to echo through time, "I don't want to hold you back." They had left a chasm in my chest, a hollow space where her laughter and light once resided.

But as we stood there, her hands finding their familiar place in my hair, I could almost laugh at the irony of it all. The heartbreak had been a crucible, forging a path that led us back to each other here on this island, where the palm trees swayed like dancers to the rhythm of the ocean's song. The past was a distant storm cloud on the horizon, its shadows giving way to the brilliant hues of the present.

"Everything makes sense now," I confessed, pulling

back just enough to drink in the sight of her—her eyes reflecting the myriad of stars overhead, her skin glowing like molten gold in the moonlight. "We were meant to be here, Piper. Everything that happened... it was all leading up to this."

As the breeze whispered secrets to the sand beneath our feet, I could feel the threads of our lives intertwining once more, creating a tapestry richer than either of us could have woven alone. In the grand tapestry of life, family and wealth paled compared to the treasure I had found in Piper's return. Her love was the compass that oriented me, and I knew without a doubt that wherever she was, that was where I belonged.

My desires had always been simple and elemental, like the waves crashing relentlessly against the shore—constant, powerful, and unapologetic. Piper embodied those yearnings; she was the voyage I longed to embark upon without a map or compass.

"Life's funny," I murmured against her lips, my breath mingling with hers. "I've sprinted across fields, chased victory beneath floodlights, yet nothing compares to this stillness, to the quiet certainty that you are where I'm meant to finish my race."

Her fingers traced the line of my jaw, a silent artist capturing moments not in sketches but in touches.

The concept of coaching lingered in my mind, unfamiliar and strangely appropriate, as if I were donning a bespoke suit meant for a future version of myself. Coaching transcended mere instruction; it delved into the realm of mentorship, urging budding athletes to surpass boundaries, discover their unique journey within the sport, and grasp the essence of authentic competition.

At that moment, as the sun bore witness to our reunion, I realised I was stepping onto an unfamiliar pitch where I could shape destinies rather than chase after a solitary ball. Piper's presence stirred a new ambition, a desire to inspire and nurture dreams the way I once pursued my own.

Feeling the weight of past aspirations shift into a pattern I hadn't expected—but one that felt right.

Our kiss deepened, as natural as breathing, as necessary as the tides. Piper's body pressed closer, arching into the contours of my own, a silent testament to the magnetic force that had always drawn us together. Her arms wound around my neck, anchoring me in the present, in the reality of her embrace.

I pulled back slightly, the taste of salt from her lips lingering as I caught my breath. Our foreheads touched, and I allowed myself to drown in the depths of Piper's green eyes, an ocean of emotions swirling within them. "You're not leaving my arms again," I said, the words rolling off my tongue with a conviction that resonated through every fibre of my being.

Her smile was like the first break of dawn after a night of endless darkness, warming me to my core. "I've spent five years with your memory haunting my every move," she confessed, her voice soft yet carrying the weight of the time we'd lost.

The gravity of her admission struck me, anchoring me in the moment. "I don't think I have the strength to pull away again," she continued, her gaze holding mine hostage. "I don't think I have the power to leave again."

"Good," I smiled back at her, feeling a surge of hope fills the spaces between us. "Because I'm not leaving this island unless you're coming with me." My words were bold, perhaps foolishly so, but they were true. I had found my place in the world, and it wasn't on some lofty podium or beneath stadium lights—it was here, beside her, wherever 'here' might be.

In that instant, I understood that our pasts didn't define us; they simply shaped our steps toward each other. As the breeze whispered secrets only the lagoon could realise, I knew there was nowhere else I belonged but with Piper— my compass, anchor, and home.

18

Piper
Twelve months later

I reflect on the whirlwind my life has become since that fateful day at the waterfall. That serendipitous encounter with Austin had changed everything. It was as if the universe had conspired to bring us back together, and we had seized the opportunity with both hands.

After that day in O'ahu, we couldn't bear to be apart again. Austin and I returned to Los Angeles together, where we began to build a life that was even more beautiful than I had dared to dream. Our bond, tested by time and distance, proved to be unbreakable.

We bought a charming house in a leafy neighbourhood that perfectly matches our tastes. With its large windows and sunlit rooms, the house felt like home when we stepped inside. We filled it with laughter, love, and memories, making it our sanctuary.

My job with the magazine continued to be a source of joy and fulfilment. I travelled frequently, capturing the essence of diverse cultures and landscapes, but no matter where my work took me, I always found my way back to Austin and our home.

The artistic freedom I had only grew, and my editorials flourished as if inspired by the happiness that permeated my life. Austin embraced his new role as the coach for the college football team with enthusiasm and dedication. His passion for the sport and his players was palpable, and he quickly became a beloved figure on campus.

His transition from player to coach was seamless, and he found immense satisfaction in mentoring young athletes, helping them hone their skills and chase their dreams. Our home was never quiet for long, so we adopted two dogs: a rambunctious Golden Retriever named Max and a sweet, gentle Labrador named Luna. They brought a new level of joy and energy into our lives, and their playful antics were a constant source of amusement and affection.

Our days were filled with a comfortable routine punctuated by unexpected delight. We took long walks with Max and Luna, explored new restaurants and cafes in LA, and often found ourselves reminiscing while looking forward to the future. We hosted friends and family, and our home became a gathering place for those we loved.

Every evening, Austin and I made it a point to sit together, sharing our thoughts and experiences of the day. Those moments of connection reinforced our bond, reminding us of our journey to get here. The love we shared was deep and unwavering, a steady flame that burned brightly despite the challenges we had faced.

I am profoundly grateful as I look around our home, filled with the warmth of love and the echoes of laughter. Austin is my anchor, my partner, and my best friend. The life we have built together is more than I ever imagined possible. Each day is a testament to our resilience, commitment, and love.

When I reflect on our journey in quiet moments, I am filled with a sense of peace and contentment. The path that led us back to each other was unexpected but brought us to enduring happiness. As we continue building our lives together, I know the best is yet to come.

As the sun dipped below the horizon, casting a warm, golden glow over our backyard, Austin and I found ourselves wrapped in the tranquility of a perfect Los Angeles evening. We had just finished a delightful dinner on the patio, accompanied by Max and Luna's playful antics. The air was filled with the scent of blooming jasmine, adding a romantic touch to the atmosphere. After tidying up, we retreated inside.

The house, dimly lit by soft ambient lights, exuded a cozy intimacy. I poured each a glass of our favourite wine, and we settled onto the plush sofa in the living room. Austin's arm wrapped around my shoulders, pulling me close. I felt his warmth, strength, and heart's steady beat. We talked about our day, sharing stories and laughter, but there was an undercurrent of something more profound. The way his eyes lingered on mine, the subtle brush of his fingers against my skin—it was as if the air between us was charged with a magnetic energy.

Austin set his glass down and turned to face me fully, his eyes intense and filled with love and desire. "Piper," he murmured, his voice husky. "Remember the cabana?" His words sent a shiver down my spine, and I felt my core heat up.

"How could I forget?" I replied, my voice soft but filled with conviction. You were such a good boy for me."

He leaned in, capturing my lips in a kiss that started tender but quickly deepened, igniting a fire within me. Our glasses were forgotten as we became lost in each other. His hands roamed over my back, pulling me closer, and I responded by threading my fingers through his hair, tugging gently. We moved together, rising from the sofa and making our way to the bedroom, our kisses never breaking.

The walk was bathed in the bright glow of the moonlight filtering through the curtains, casting a serene, almost magical light. Austin lifted me into his arms on the stairs, my legs tightly around his middle. He pushed my back against the wall, pressing his hard erection against my heat, and I had to whimper into his mouth.

His tongue lapped up every noise I made. Austin's touch was both gentle and possessive as he undressed me, his eyes never leaving mine. Every caress and every kiss was a testament to the depth of our connection. When we were finally free of our clothes, he pulled me onto the bed, his body pressing against mine.

"I'll show you how good I can be for you." He said in a rough but determined voice. His mouth trailed down my throat to the swell of my breasts, his teeth tugging gently at my hard and sensitive peaks. I felt my arousal pooling between my legs and rolled my hips in anticipation against Austin's cock.

He moved further down, and when he reached my core, my back arched off the mattress, my mind exploding with fireworks. Austin slid his tongue between my folds, and when he made contact with my bundle of nerves, I was done for. His sweet assault on me drove me higher and higher. But then he stopped abruptly, looking up at me, his mouth covered in my arousal.

"No cumming until I tell you." My head fell back onto the mattress, knowing fully what he was up to—the sweetest torture.

Every time I was close, my legs quivering around Austin's head, jolts of electricity pulsing through my veins, he stopped. I was on the brink of losing my mind, my fingers digging hard into our sheets.

"Austin, please," I begged, my voice laced with desperate need.

"Please what, Piper?" he mockingly asked. My breaths were already coming in quick succession, my insides on fire. He could've demanded anything from me at this moment.

"Let me cum, please. Sir!" I spat out, willing to give him everything he asked for. His hands shifted under my thighs, moving to my overworked pussy and spreading me as wide as possible.

Before his mouth descended on me once more, he looked into my eyes and whispered, "Good girl." It took all but thirty seconds for Austin's slick and skilled tongue to push me over the edge. My moans echoed off the walls and throughout the house. Every fibre in me tingled with my release's beautiful sensations, and Austin did not miss a drop.

He let me recover for a moment before climbing back over me. His cock bouncing with readiness, eager to stretch me in utmost pleasure. His face hovered over mine for a moment with a smug smile gracing his lips, knowing how good he was to me.

He entered me with one deep thrust, my eyes rolling into the back of my head. He was bigger than any man I had before, hitting all my sweet spots in one stroke. At first, his movements were slow and deliberate, but the more he chased his release, the more relentless he got. Pounding into me with all his might and before long, we both filled the room with our moans as we both found our release.

Afterward, we lay entwined, our bodies still humming with the afterglow. Austin's fingers traced lazy patterns on my skin, and I nestled closer, feeling a profound contentment.

"I love you, Piper," he whispered soothingly.

"I love you too," I replied, my voice filled with emotion. "Forever."

Our love was a force that had withstood the test of time and age, and it would continue to grow, carrying us through the years with the same passion and devotion we felt tonight.

Austin

SITTING IN MY LA COLLEGE FOOTBALL HEADQUARTERS office, I leaned back in my chair and glanced at the framed photos on my desk. One photo shows Piper and me at the waterfall in O'ahu with a few of our dogs, Max and Luna, and several with my old teammates, Killian and Matt.

Coaching the college team was a dream come true, and I loved every minute of it, but sometimes, I missed the adrenaline rush of being on the field as a player. My thoughts drifted back to when the three of us dominated the field. Killian, with his lightning-fast speed and uncanny ability to read the game, and Matt, with his brute strength and unyielding determination. We had shared countless victories, defeats, and unforgettable moments on and off the field.

They were both still thriving in their professional careers while I had transitioned to coaching. Killian had just come off a stellar season, leading his team to the play-offs and earning himself MVP. On the other hand, Matt was known as the league's most formidable linebacker, with a reputation for stopping even the most elusive running backs in their tracks.

Despite their success, they always found time to catch up with me, reminiscing about the old days and sharing our latest exploits. Today was one of those days. We had planned to meet at our favourite restaurant downtown, a cozy spot where the staff knew us by name and the food was consistently excellent.

The familiar scent of sizzling steaks and freshly baked bread greeted me as I walked in. I spotted Killian and Matt at our usual table, already engaged in a heated discussion about the latest game.

"Hey, look who finally decided to show up," Matt teased as I approached. "Thought you might've gotten lost on your way here."

"Funny, Matt," I replied with a grin, clapping him on the back. "Good to see you both."

Killian leaned back in his chair, a mischievous glint in his eye. "So, Coach Austin, how's it going with the college team? Heard you've got some promising recruits this year."

"Yeah, things are going great," I said, sitting. "We've got a solid lineup, and the kids are eager to learn. It's a different kind of challenge, but I love it. How about you guys? How's life in the big leagues treating you?"

Killian chuckled. "Well, it's not without its ups and downs. The media can be a pain, but there's nothing like the thrill of a live game. Plus, winning MVP didn't hurt." Matt nodded in agreement.

"Yeah, and crushing opponents week after week is pretty satisfying. But we do miss having you on the field with us, man. It's not the same without our ace quarterback."

"I miss it too," I admitted. "There's nothing quite like the roar of the crowd and the rush of the game. But coaching gives me a new perspective. I get to shape these young athletes and watch them grow. It's rewarding in its way."

We continued chatting, exchanging stories and laughs, the camaraderie as strong as ever. Eventually, the conversation became more personal, and I knew it was time to drop the bombshell.

"Speaking of personal lives," I began, trying to keep my tone casual, "I've got something I need your advice on." Killian and Matt both leaned in, intrigued.

"Oh? This sounds serious," Killian said, his eyebrows raised.

I took a deep breath, feeling a mix of excitement and nervousness. "Well, you guys know how much Piper means to me. We've been together for over a year, and I've never been happier. So, I've been thinking… I want to ask her to marry me."

The End

Read on for the first chapter of book 2 in this series.

WICKED BONDS

J.N. KING & CASSANDRA DOON

CHAPTER ONE

BELLADONNA

HIM´s "Buried Alive by Love" is blaring through my car so loudly, the driver next to me at the traffic lights is throwing some amazed looks my way.

Something I've gotten used to, but I chuckle, nonetheless. I portray the perfect image of a corporate business-woman, wearing my white blouse, with my dark hair pinned up, and the Range Rover, I look anything but who I am on the inside. Deep down, my heart loves the darkness. In high school, my circle of friends were emos, goths, metal heads, and punks.

My eyeliner was the blackest black available, with fishnets, that were ripped at my thighs, and rugged combat boots; that were well and truly worn. I spent my weekends at sweaty underground venues, watching bands play music; that would have made my grandmother cry. But it was my world, my love, until adulthood forced me to conform to the expected standard.

However, I've managed to find the perfect balance. At night, with my black hair and eyeliner, I still attend gigs.

My apartment furniture and decor has mainly been sourced from antique stores and the Halloween sections of stores close to me. During the day, I am a quite successful businesswoman, which means I also look the part.

Today, nothing could have soured my great mood. It's the kickoff for Halloween shenanigans, at our local theme park. Every year for the last three years, the theme park puts on an incredible Halloween scare fest. Complete with scare mazes, actors, shows, and everything horror themed. I zoom through the streets to get home; I need to get ready. I still need to shower and change into something more... appropriate. I'll be meeting up with my best friend, Cora. So, we can make our way to the park on time. She too has a love for Halloween, even if it is more the cozy side of Halloween, but she loves the spooky stuff, nonetheless.

I park in my designated spot and head into the elevator, pressing the fifth floor. I enter my apartment, kicking my heels off as I head straight for the shower. An hour later, I look at my reflection in the mirror and smile. My amber eyes are adorned with faint red and purple eyeshadow and lined with a black cat-eye style outline; complemented by a deep burgundy shade on my plump lips. My outfit consists of a skintight black, knee-length skirt, that I have paired with a cropped black and purple HIM band tee, and my shiny combat boots.

As I put my choker on around my delicate neck, the excitement of tonight and the weekend ahead is running through me in waves. It's times like this, that I don't regret being single at the age of 32. Less than a year ago, I got out of a long-term relationship and am finally finding my footing again.

My ex-Trevor wasn't a bad guy and essentially, that is what drove us apart. He was the sweetest guy, a veterinarian, who was so chill and laid back, He took me out on dates and also loved movie nights; the kind of ones where you cuddle up on the sofa. It's not that I didn't like that, because I did, but I also really like to—and I mean really —get fucked hard in the bedroom, and poor Trevor, well he really just loved sweet vanilla style sex. I was always left feeling unsatisfied, and when he asked if we should take the next step in our relationship, and move in together, well, I couldn't help but run for the hills. It wasn't just the sex; cute sex is essential after all. He could never fully accept me, for who I am deep down. When he asked me to move in with him, he made it clear that my taste in home decor was distasteful to him, and I would definitely have to get rid of it.

Essentially, change who I am, to fit his checkbox.

Yeah, no thanks, Sir. Next.

This isn't just a phase in my life, it's my lifestyle. I will never give up who I am for a guy. Especially if said guy, is so vanilla in bed.

Life is too short, to not go for what you want. Never settle for less than you deserve.

I grab my vintage leather jacket off the hook by the front door and head back down to my car. As I enter the elevator, I press the button to descend to the garage. I pull my long black hair into a high ponytail. The doors open and I exit the elevator, Giddy excitement courses through me with my hair swinging happily from side to side with each step, as I make my way over to my parking spot.

The drive is fairly quick considering the time of the

day, the traffic usually plagues this area and its normally longer. I pre-ordered a reserved parking spot, close to the south entrance, as I pull in, I spot Cora, who is already waiting for me.

She's wearing her infamous black and white striped leggings, with a Beetlejuice top, that is tied in a knot at her waist; giving it a cropped vibe, and plateau Mary Jane's. Her dark blonde shoulder-length hair is in a side braid. She's single too now, after she recently caught her ex-husband cheating on her, with an old college friend.

He's such a waste of space; they had even been planning to have kids. But we've gotten through it all, together. I've known the girl since we were six years old. We instantly knew we were platonic Soulmates.

She struts over to me, the second I begin to get out of my car. "Evening girl, I could hear your music from two blocks away." Her green eyes light up, a smile tugs at the corner of her lips. I give her my best Cheshire cat grin and with our arms linked like schoolgirls, we make our way over to the busy entrance.

The atmosphere is electric from the moment we walk into the park. We step through the gates, and instantly, everything feels different. The usual upbeat music has been replaced by creepy, haunting sounds that send a chill up my spine. I can hear distant screams, and the air feels heavy with fog rolling along the ground. The lights are dim, casting long, eerie shadows, and the usual bright colours of the park have been swapped for dark, twisted decorations. There are people in costumes everywhere, some actors, and others just trying to blend in; but all of them add to the strange vibe.

I catch a glimpse of a scare maze up ahead, its entrance is guarded by towering, sinister looking figures. The whole place seems alive with apprehension, as if something is just waiting to jump out at me. I can't help but smile, this is exactly what I came here for, the thrill from my periphery, I spot some scare actors. I never quite know how to act when they approach—it seems unfit to show that it's their presence that excites me the most.

I've always had a mask kink and being here just intensifies that primal feeling. Back in my last year of high school, my then-boyfriend Dean was on the same sexual wavelength as me. We explored our likes and wants, pushing our limits, and always craving more. But as soon as we were in our first year of university, each on the other side of the state, we drifted apart. Ever since then, despite the people I surround myself with, I have never found another sexual partner that ticks the boxes I crave.

I feel the hair on the back of my neck rise, as a presence behind us rips me from my thoughts. Lo and behold, a scare actor sneak up from behind us, and Cora jump a few paces away from me with a surprised shriek. I turn, waiting for the awareness to settle in, but before I can make eye contact with the person who looks like a butcher from a horror movie, with blood-smeared apron, mangled mask, and cleaver in hand; he moves back into the shadows. I reach for Cora's hand, and we venture further into the night.

After the third maze, I am in desperate need of coffee, Cora and I decide on a small booth selling drinks and snacks, that looks so out of place amidst the Halloween horrors going on around us. It has two small tables and a few chairs in front, we manage to get one, so we can sit down and relax for a little while.

I don't easily scare, but this year they have ramped up the scare factor in these mazes, and gosh, even I have jumped out of my skin a few times.

"They've outdone themselves this year, I think I've nearly shat my pants a few times," Cora declares with laughter in between gulps of her iced latte, she's using a straw so she can try not to smear her black lipstick, her green eyes gleaming.

"They did, even I've come close and that's unheard of?!" We both laugh, enjoying our night to the fullest. We finish our drinks, and before we head back into the dark chaos, I head to the restroom, leaving Cora safely behind at the table. I weave my way through the throngs of people, following the illuminated signs for toilets, when the hairs on my neck stand up once again.

Someone is behind me.

Closer than they should be.

ABOUT J.N. KING

Born and raised in Germany, to an English mother and German father, J N started writing romance short stories for her school paper as a teenager. Over the years, she wrote several unpublished books in German and English as a hobby. She now writes full-time, inspired by the rainy days in England, that is if she isn't daydreaming about the books she reads.

J N now resides in England, with her family.

ALSO BY J.N. KING

Out Now:

The Boys Of Hastings House

His Majesty

The Waterfall

Bittersweet Snapdragon

Aces

Veada

Wicked Bonds

Coming soon:

The Restaurant

The Crimson Crown

Nailah

ABOUT CASSANDRA DOON

Cassandra Doon hails from New South Wales, Australia, where she was nurtured between the bustling streets of Sydney and the serene snowy mountains of Tumut. Today, she finds inspiration in the breathtaking Scenic Rim of Queensland's Gold Coast. A versatile author with a lifelong passion for storytelling, Cassandra has penned over 26 novels and 5 children's books, exploring a variety of genres. Known for her daydreaming and a head often lost in the clouds, she admits to being more at home in her fictional worlds than on social media. Outside of her literary pursuits, Cassandra is a devoted mother to two boys, dedicating her days to their endless energy as both a soccer mom and Pokémon master.

Standalone:

The Kings of Willows Peak

Damaged Goods

Tuesday May

The Devils Cut

The Detectives Mate

Dark Dahlias Rite

A Field of Tulips and Bones

Follow Poppy

To Her

Blood moon

Unit 9

Broken Creek Ranch

Eclipsion (Coming Soon)

The Dead Zone (Coming Soon)

* * *

Oakland Harbour Series:

Missing

Found

Home

* * *

The Boys Series

The Boys Of Hastings House

The Boys of Bittersweet College

The Boys of Nightsbane Academy (Coming Soon)

The Boys of Winchester U (Coming Soon)

* * *

Second Chances Series:

The Waterfall

Wicked Bonds

Writhe (Coming Soon)

The Restaurant (Coming Soon)

* * *

Umbravivus Series:

The Lost Kingdom of Umbravivus (Coming Soon)

The Crowned King of Umbravivus (Coming Soon)

The Queen of Umbravivus (Coming Soon)

* * *

Butcher and the Witch Series:

Poison is always in the Prettiest Bottle

Candles make Great Alibis

Socials with a Slice of Pie

Also By C.L. Doon

The Rain Dang Detective Series:

Still Waters

Moving Waters (coming Soon)

Standalone:

Second Chances at The Riverbend Café

Lavender (Coming Soon)

Also By C. Doon

Standalone:

Ravenwood Manor

Phantom Navis